IN THE DAYS OF ALFRED THE GREAT

This edition published 2023
by Living Book Press
Copyright © Living Book Press, 2023

ISBN: 978-1-76153-998-5 (hardcover)
        978-1-76153-001-2 (softcover)

First published in 1900.

All rights reserved. No part of this publication may be reproduced, stored in a retrieval system, or transmitted in any other form or means – electronic, mechanical, photocopying, recording or otherwise, without the prior permission of the copyright owner and the publisher or as provided by Australian law.

A catalogue record for this book is available from the National Library of Australia

In the Days of Alfred the Great

by

EVA MARCH TAPPAN

Contents

1.	Alfred's Early Home	1
2.	Life on the Manor	11
3.	Alfred Goes to London	24
4.	Across the Continent	36
5.	"My Pope"	47
6.	Ethelbald's Revolt	59
7.	Queen Judith	71
8.	Who Shall Be King?	82
9.	After the Massacre	94
10.	On the Island of Thanet	107
11.	"I Must Serve My People"	118
12.	The Coming of the Sons of Lodbrog	130
13.	The Danes at Croyland	142
14.	The White Horse of Ashdown	154
15.	Thor or Thealfi?	167
16.	In Time of Peace	180

Chapter I.

ALFRED'S EARLY HOME

The palace in which Alfred the Great was born was hardly what we should call a palace in these days. It was a long, low, wooden house, or rather a group of houses; for whenever more room was needed, a new building was put up, and joined to the old ones wherever it seemed most convenient, so that the palace looked much like a company of one-story houses that had drifted together in a flood. There had to be room for a large family, for the king's counsellors and many of the church dignitaries lived with him. All around the house were many smaller houses for the fighting and the working men. Those were the days when at any moment a messenger might come flying on a panting horse and say:—

"O King Ethelwulf, the Danes are upon us! Their ships are in the offing, and they are driving toward Thanet."

Then the king would send horsemen in hot haste to all his underchiefs, and he himself, at the head of the soldiers of his household, would march toward the coast, sometimes to fight and sometimes, if fighting failed, to buy them off by a ransom of money and jewels and vessels of gold and of silver.

The priests, with the women and children, would hasten into the church and throw themselves down before the altar and pray:—

"From the fury of the Northmen, good Lord, deliver us."

They had good reason for their alarm; for perhaps even before the king and his men could reach the eastern shore, another fleet would come to land on the southern coast, and the fierce Danes would sweep like a whirlwind through the land, burning the homes of the people, carrying away the women, and tossing the little children back and forth on the points of their spears.

There were many workingmen about the king's palace, for almost everything that was needed had to be made on the premises. Not only must the grain be raised, wheat or barley or oats or corn, but it must be ground, sometimes by many small hand-mills, and sometimes by one large mill that belonged to the king. For drink, there was a kind of mead, or ale, and that must be brewed in the king's brewery. When it came to the question of clothes, there was still more work to do; for leather must be tanned for the shoes as well as for the harnesses, and flax and wool must be spun and woven. Then, too, there were blacksmiths, who not only made the simple implements needed to carry on the farm, but who must be skilful enough to make and repair the metal network of the coats of mail, and to keep the soldiers well supplied with spears and swords and battle-axes and arrowheads.

A king who was willing to "rough it" a little could live on his royal domain very comfortably without sending away for many luxuries. If his land did not border on the seashore, he would have to send for salt that was made by evaporating sea-water; and whenever he needed a mill-stone, he would send to France, for the best ones were found in quarries near Paris. For iron, King Ethelwulf sent to Sussex, not a very long journey, to be sure, but by no means an easy one, for some of the roads were of the roughest kind. If he had lived on the coast, it would have been almost as easy to send to Spain for iron, and sometimes men did make the long voyage rather than go a much shorter distance by land and bring home the heavy load. When the millstones were landed from France, the laborers had to take their cattle, and make the slow, tiresome journey to the shore to bring them home.

All these things were very interesting for the little Prince Alfred to see, though he was not quite five years old at the time when this story begins. He was the youngest child of King Ethelwulf and Queen Osburga, and a favorite with everybody on the great estate. The blacksmith had made him a tiny coat of mail and a spear, and he and the other children would play "Fight the Danes," and the soldiers would look on and say, "There's a prince for you," and often one of them would take him up before him on his horse for a mad gallop through the forest. The half-wild swine would scatter before them, and sometimes the soldier, holding the little boy firmly with one hand, would charge upon them, and leaning far over the saddle, would run his spear through one; and back they would ride to the palace, dragging the pig behind them, and the little prince, his long, yellow hair streaming in the wind, would shout, "A Dane, father! We have killed a Dane!"

Nobody troubled the little boy about learning to read. Priests must read, of course, both English and Latin, for the service of the church was in Latin, and they must know how to pronounce the words, though very few of them were quite sure what the words meant. Kings seldom learned anything of books, but King Ethelwulf could read, for when he was a young man he had wished to become a priest and had studied a little with this plan in mind. His father had opposed the scheme; for after the older brother's death Ethelwulf was his only son, and there was no one else to whom he could leave the kingdom. He was greatly troubled, for he was afraid that a king who could read would not be a good warrior, but he finally decided to test him by giving him a small kingdom to practise on; so he put Kent into his hands, and for ten years Ethelwulf ruled under his father's eye. He was so attentive to his duties as a king, that his father concluded that learning how to read had not hurt him, and so at his death he left him the whole kingdom.

Even if no one made the little boy learn to read, the days were never long enough for him. The great domain was a busy place. Everybody was making something, and everybody was glad to have the little prince look on and ask questions. There were hives of bees, and there were hunting dogs and hawks. People were coming and going from morning till night. The king rented much of his land to different families. He was bound to care for them, and they were bound to fight under him and to work for him, to make hedges and ditches, to plough, to shear the sheep, and to help make roads. Besides this, they were to pay him rent, and this rent seldom came in money, but rather in produce of the land. There was a steward whose business it was to receive the rent, and a boy would be interested to keep by his side all day long and watch what the people brought. There might be cheese or bacon or honey or home-brewed ale; and often there was quite a lively time when a man appeared with hens or ducks or geese, cackling or quacking or hissing, as the case might be, and all making as much noise as their throats would permit. Sometimes this rent was paid only as a token that the land belonged to the king, and had no real value. One man was bound to present three fishes fresh from the river four times a year, and another had only to bring a sheaf of wheat on a certain day of each year.

At the regular times for paying rent, these people were coming and going all day long, and often they brought besides their rent some special gift for the boy—a bag of apples or of nuts, or a particularly yellow honeycomb on a great platter of bark covered with fresh green leaves. There were all these things going on as a matter of course, but sometimes there would be heard the trampling of hoofs and a great cry, and all the men who had been paying their rent, and all the men who were working in the fields, and all the servants of the house would run out and cry:—

"Hillo! What ho?" and the men who had been hunting would ride into the little settlement, dragging behind them a wild boar or a deer to be roasted on the great hearth in the hall.

Alfred was, as I said, the youngest of King Ethelwulf's five children. His sister, Ethelswitha, was only eleven years older than he, and she was his special friend. He was not very strong, and there were days when he liked better to stay in the house and listen to her stories than even to be among all the interesting things that were going on outside. One day she began:—

"Once there was a king, and he built a great hall—"

"My father's a king," said the little boy. "Was the hall like ours?"

"Oh, it was larger and much finer; but when the men were asleep in it, a monster used to come and carry them off to a cave under the water and eat them. At last a great warrior came, and he killed the dragon, and the water was all red with his blood."

"My brother Ethelbald would kill a dragon; he fought in a real battle," said Alfred. "Tell me more about the man that killed the dragon."

"The king gave him rings and bracelets and spears and shields, and he went home to his own people; and by and by some one told him of another dragon that lived in a cave in the land, and had gold vases and spears and bronze shields and gold rings for the neck and for the arms; and he went out to kill this dragon so as to give the gold to the men."

"Did he go alone?"

"No, his fighting men went with him; but when the dragon came, it breathed out fire, and they were afraid, and all but one of them ran away from him."

"I would have stayed," said the little prince.

"And so I believe you would," said King Ethelwulf, who had been listening to their talk. "You would fight; but women do not fight; and what would you do, Ethelswitha, for a brave man?"

"I would pass him the mead as my mother does, and when you gave him great gifts, I would put the rings on his arms and the necklace about his neck, and he would say: 'It is the daughter of my king that gives me this, and I will fight for my king. My body and blood shall be his.' "

"Good, my girl. That you have done for many of my brave men; but if it was a great warrior who had fought beside your father, a warrior who was a king? Could you do no more for him?" And he looked closely into the eyes of the young girl.

"What else could I do, father?" she asked. "You never told me to do anything more for your thegns, and no one can be braver than they."

The king looked a little puzzled, then he said:—

"Come here, Alfred, and I'll tell you a story, and Ethelswitha may listen."

"About the brave king?" asked Alfred.

"Yes, about the brave king," said his father. "The brave king lives to the north of us, in Mercia. His name is Buhred. The Welsh people who live beyond him kept coming into his country, and when they came they would steal the treasures and kill the people."

"Did they eat them, too?"

"No," said the king, "but they tormented them, and shot them with arrows, and stabbed them with short, strong knives. This king was very brave, but he had not men enough to drive them away, so he sent to me and asked if I would help him. I think you can remember when we rode away from here."

"Mother and you and I went to the church, Alfred," said his sister, "to pray that they might come home safely."

"Yes, I remember," and the little boy nodded wisely.

"Well, this king had not any wife, but his sister went to their church and prayed for him to come back to her. He was very strong and killed a great many men, and the bad Welsh were all driven away, and then he went home. He wished that he had a wife at home to greet him, and he asked me if I would give him my daughter."

Alfred had slipped down from his father's knee, but the king put his arm about his daughter, who was sitting on the bench beside him, and said:—

"Do you see now what you can do for him?"

The young girl looked straight into her father's eyes, and said:—

"Is he as brave a man as you?"

"Yes," said the king.

"Then I will be his wife," said she.

This was a few months before the time of our story, and the little boy had, of course, forgotten the conversation, but the wedding and the wedding feast even so little a fellow as he was could not forget.

Ever since Ethelswitha was a little child, the queen and the maidens of the household had been preparing for her marriage. They had spun and woven great chests full of linen and woolen. They had made beautifully embroidered tapestries and rich coverings for the benches of the hall. They had made gowns of blue and red and yellow and green, whose deep borders were worked with silk and with threads of gold. Then there were wide mantles of all the colors of the rainbow for her to wear over her gown. They were wound about the waist and thrown over the left shoulder, and they were so long that they would fall down nearly to the ground. These, too, were richly embroidered with gold thread. Both Queen Osburga and King Ethelwulf were descendants of Cerdic, who had conquered the Isle of Wight three hundred years before this. Some of their kinsfolk still dwelt near the island, and were skilful workers in gold and silver. From there had been brought beautiful ornaments, clasps for the cloak, necklaces, and ear-rings. One of the clasps was circular in shape, made of a fine gold filigree work. The centre was filled by a double star set with garnets. Another clasp was of silver in the shape of a Maltese cross, with green enamel around the edges and a ruby in the centre. Then there was a necklace with many gold pendants and a blue stone in each. There were "stick-pins" of red and blue enamel, and there were ear-rings of precisely the crescent shape that our grandmothers used to wear.

The king had houses in several places and went from one to another as the needs of his kingdom demanded. Sometimes there would be fear of an attack by the Danes or the Welsh, for which the presence of the king might help his people to prepare. Sometimes there was a new church to be dedicated in some distant part of the kingdom, and then the furniture, the tapestries, and the valuable dishes were put on pack-horses, and thither the king and his great family would go, and stay for a few weeks or months, as the case might be. Then there was another reason, perhaps the strongest of all. The king was really "boarded around." There was not a great deal of money in the kingdom, and the easiest way to collect rent was to eat it in the shape of the grain and vegetables that the tenants brought in; so the king and his court would stay till they had eaten the products of the land in one place, and would then move on to another. The queen liked especially the house at Chippenham in Wiltshire, and so it was decided that there the marriage should be celebrated. The palace was in a beautiful valley through which the Avon flowed. Other streams were near, and the rolling country around was rich with fresh green forests.

King Buhred came marching up with a great company of his men at arms, and King Ethelwulf stood ready to receive him. It was a brilliant sight, with the background of the woods and the river and the low-lying hills. King Ethelwulf was in advance of his men and was mounted on a great white horse. He wore a rich purple tunic, and over it a short blue cloak with a gold border. This was fastened at the shoulder with a gold brooch flashing with red stones. Bands of bright-colored cloth were wound about his legs, and ended in tassels at the knee.

On the saddle before him was the little prince, his yellow hair flying over a scarlet tunic; and next behind them came the three older sons of the king, wearing yellow tunics and blue cloaks.

Then came the bishops and priests with their vestments of white and gold, and behind them were King Ethelwulf's fighting men, with their light blue tunics, whose borders were embroidered with leaves and circles. Their short cloaks were fastened on the right shoulder or under the chin by a clasp. They carried shields and spears that flashed in the sun as they marched.

The queen wore a long red gown with wide-hanging sleeves. Her mantle of purple hung over her left shoulder in graceful folds.

The young bride, who was only fifteen, wore a white gown and white mantle, and her hair was bound by a narrow gold fillet set with blue stones. It must have been a gorgeous scene in the great hall of feasting. Iron lamps hung from the rafters and shone down upon the bright spears and helmets and chain armor that hung upon the walls. Brave deeds of their ancestors were pictured in the tapestry. In the centre of the hall was a great fireplace, or hearth, made of burnt clay, where the meat was roasted. Long tables were spread down the hall, and at the upper end was a platform where the royal family sat, and a few of the thegns whom the king wished to honor.

All day and far into the night was the feasting kept up, till even in the midst of the rejoicing little Alfred fell asleep in his father's arms. He was awakened by a sudden silence, and then came the sound of singing and of playing on the harp; for the harpers were come in their long green gowns and gay mantles, and all the brave warriors were silent listening to their music, for the one thing that they enjoyed most was to have a harper come in after the feast was well begun and sing to them the ballads of their people.

Long it lasted, but the time came when even the merriest of them had had enough of merriment, and the feast was ended.

Queen Osburga was sad at losing her only daughter, and she clasped the little Alfred more closely than ever to her breast, and kissed him again and again. The king was silent, and as she looked up, she saw his eyes fixed upon her and Alfred with a strange expression of pity and suffering and determination.

"What is it, my husband?" she asked, fearful of something she knew not what.

"Perhaps it is nothing. They say that the thought is clearer in the morning light. We will sleep now, and when the sun rises, I will think. Sleep well, my own true wife."

The king looked sad and troubled, and Osburga lay with a burden on her heart, she knew not what, even till the sun rose over the forest.

Chapter II.

LIFE ON THE MANOR

Ethelswitha was gone, and Alfred was lonely, though his nurse Hilda, who was always with him, roamed about wherever he chose to go. They were wandering idly about the place when suddenly they heard shouting and screaming. Men were striking stones together and beating bits of iron, and all the small boys of the settlement were adding to the noise in every way that they could.

"It is the bees," said Hilda. "Look! See them in the air!" And there they were flying in a dense swarm, slowly and in a vague, uncertain fashion. At last they seemed to rest on their wings almost motionless. The men drew back a little and looked at Hilda. She stepped forward, and caught up a handful of gravel in each hand. That in the left she threw over her left shoulder. Holding her right hand straight up above her head, she looked at the bees, tossed the rest of the gravel into the midst of them, and said in a kind of chanting tone:—

> "Lithe and listen, my lady-bees;
> Fly not far to the forest trees."

The moment that her voice was still, the noise began again louder than ever. The bees slowly settled down upon the limb of a tree in a shining, quivering mass. A hive made of braided straw was rubbed out with fresh leaves and put over them, and the swarm was safe.

"The old charms have not lost their power," said Hilda to the blacksmith.

"No, that they have not," said the blacksmith, "but they will not work for every one."

"The king's religion is the true one, of course, and we are baptized and go to his church, but the old gods are angry if we do not remember them sometimes," said Hilda. "The Christian God is good and kind, but the old gods will often work one harm, and it is just as well to say a good word to them now and then. You can say a prayer in the church afterwards."

The smith picked up the heavy tongs that he had been beating to add to the din, and went across the open place to where Alfred stood gazing curiously at the beehives.

"Will it please you, sir prince," he said, "to come to the forge? To-day I have finished my work on the king's new sword. Will you see it?"

"Yes, I will," said Alfred, and they walked down to the little valley where the forge stood. As they crossed the brook, swollen by the recent rains, Hilda hurried the little boy over the narrow foot-bridge.

"Be careful," she said, "and never look down at the water, for that is where the black nixy-man lives. He is angry when children look at him, and he snaps at them, and drags them down and eats them." So they went on till they came to the rude hut in which the smith had built his great fire on a heavy stone hearth. The sword was brought out, but Alfred was disappointed to see that it did not shine.

"My father's sword shines," he said at last.

"So will this," said the smith, "but first it must go to the goldworker, and he will polish it and twist gold cord about the handle, and put bands of bronze about it—and perhaps he will get a wise man to cut a rune into it," he whispered to Hilda.

"The king would not be pleased," said she.

"But it might save his life," said the smith. "Did you never hear of the two kings, Jarl and Thorl, how they fought; and each was a great warrior, and at the first stroke each drove his sword clear through the body of the other? Thorl's armorer loved him, and he had secretly had a rune cut on the inside of the handle where the king would never see it; but Jarl's armorer hated him, and so there was no rune on his sword; and the men stood, each with the other's sword run clear through him. But Jarl's sword sprang out from Thorl's body, and no one ever saw it again, and the wound closed, and there was no scar. But Thorl's sword had a rune on it, and so it did not spring out of the wound. It grew heavier and heavier, and in a minute Jarl sank down and died."

Alfred and Hilda had seated themselves under a tree not far from the great rock that stood beside the little hut of the smith. Alfred said:—

"Hilda, what is a rune?"

"It's a strange mark," said Hilda. "Long ago, when the gods used to live with men, they told a few very wise men how to make these signs. The gods know what they mean, and if a man cuts them on his sword, then the gods will come to help him when he fights; but you must not tell the bishop, for the priests do not like the runes."

"Are they afraid of them? Is the runes' god stronger than their God?" asked Alfred.

"No, I suppose not," said Hilda, a little doubtfully, "but they will not let us use them."

Alfred thought a minute, and then said:—

"Was Thorl a good man?"

"Yes," said Hilda.

"If Jarl had been a good man, would not his sword have stayed in as well as Thorl's?"

"I don't know," said Hilda, a little hastily, and looked around over her shoulder, for she was not a little afraid of the evil spirits that she believed were in the air all around. Then, too, she had just seen an eagle fly by toward the left, and she knew that this was a bad sign.

"Come a little way into the forest," she said, "and we will gather flowers, and I will make you a crown, because some day you will have a crown of gold and sit on the high seat on the dais; and you will ride at the head of the fighting men when they go out to battle, and when they speak to you, they will bow down low and say, 'Hail, sir king.' "

They wandered on and on into the forest, for Hilda was thoughtless of danger except from evil spirits. At last they sat down on a mossy log to rest, and Alfred said:—

"Tell me a story about a king," and Hilda began:—

"Once upon a time there was a king, and he was an old man—"

"Was he as old as my father?"

"Much older," said Hilda. "He was so old that he knew that he must soon die, and he told the thegns to build him a beautiful boat. They must paint it white and put a broad band of gold around it, and the sails must be of gold woven into cloth. At the bow was a pillar made of wood and gilded; and on the pillar was an image of a mighty warrior, and this warrior was a great god."

"Did he use to live with men?" asked the boy.

"Yes, but it was so long ago that no one can remember his name," said Hilda.

"Perhaps if we knew his name and cut it on all the swords, the

Danes would never dare to come to the land again," said Alfred. At this, Hilda looked a little frightened, for she had been forbidden to tell the prince of the heathen gods; but the child went on:—

"How did he look? Did he look like my father?"

"No one could ever see his face without dying," said Hilda, "but his helmet covered it, so people could come near and bow down at his feet and make him presents. He had a blue banner in his right hand, and a great red rose was embroidered on it. The crest of his helmet was a cock, and on his shield was a lion with flowers around his neck."

"You haven't made my crown," said Alfred. "Make it, for I shall be a king; and tell me what this king did."

So Hilda wove a wreath of the pretty scarlet anemones and put it on the boy's head, and went on with her story.

"The king told his men to hang all around the outside of his vessel the shields that he had used, and behind every shield they were to put three spears fastened together with golden chains; and on the mast was the most beautiful shield of all, the one that the king had carried in his greatest battle, and over it was his banner, blood-red, with a bear in the centre. And at the stern of the vessel was the king's coat of mail, and it flashed like fire when the sun shone on it. Then the king bade his men to pile up a great heap of dry pine wood on the ship in front of the figure, and over that to put fir, and over that oak, and to bind it with golden chains, and to hang golden chains from the masts, and to put many jeweled rings on the prow. Men wondered what it might mean, but they must obey the king, and so when he said:—

" 'Lay me upon your shields, and carry me on board the ship,' they did so. Then he said:—

" 'Place me on top of the oaken wood, and put my sword into

my right hand, and the chain from the helmet of the god into my left, and bind the helm straight for the north, and leave me.'

"The thegns obeyed with wonder and fear and great sorrow, and they left the ship and rowed for the shore; and they said afterward that they heard a sound like strange music and like the marching of soldiers a great way off, but before they had come to the shore, a strong wind arose from the south. Only one of the thegns dared to look at the vessel, and never until he was about to die did he tell what he saw. Then he said that he saw the king wave his sword. It made strange runes of fire in the air, and the wood of the pile began to smoke. Then the king pulled the golden chain that hung from the helmet and looked straight up into the face of the great figure; and the figure took the king by the hand. All at once it was twilight, and afar off there was a red glare on the waters; and then it was dark, and the thegns—"

"That's a good story, woman," said one of three men who suddenly appeared from among the rocks behind them, "but we can't wait to hear another"; and he bound the trembling Hilda fast with withes, while another caught up the prince.

"There'll be a fine ransom for him," said the man. "He's the son of some noble."

"Put me down. If I had my father's sword, I would run it straight through you," said the little boy.

"And who is your father?" asked the third man, while the others listened eagerly.

"My father is the king," said the child, "and I shall be a king some day—don't you see my crown?—and my father will kill you."

"Does he say true?" whispered one, in awe. "See the silver thread around his tunic. This game is too high for us. Fly! I hear the tread of horses," and the man set the child down carefully, and the three all slid into the dark shadows of the forest, leaving

Hilda lying bound. The hoof-beats grew louder, and four of the king's hunters drew near.

"It is the prince," said one, "and where is Hilda?"

"There," said another, "and bound. Who has done this? Grant that the prince be not harmed; it would kill the king."

Hilda was quickly freed, and she and the boy were put on two of the horses, which were led by two men toward the palace.

"I'll never go back to the king with such a tale," said one.

"I will," said another, "and the heads of the thieves shall go with it. How dared they venture so near the homes of the fighters of the king!" And so the two set off, and when they returned late that night, they were a grim sight, for their clothes were dusty and torn and bloody, and they held the heads of the three robbers high in the air on the points of their spears.

"We were two, but two thegns of King Ethelwulf can well meet three thieves," said they. "We smoked them out of their cave like bees from a honey tree, and they will not bind women again." The next day the three heads were carried afar into the forest and put up each on the top of a high pole, that all the other robbers might see and take warning.

Hilda was punished severely for her carelessness, and never again was the prince left in her charge. Indeed, Queen Osburga could hardly bear to have him out of her sight for a moment; and when it was found out that Hilda had been telling him the stories that she was forbidden to tell, then the king banished her from his court and sent her to a convent a long way off.

The queen was anxious about the king in those days, for he often seemed lost in thought, and many times she saw his eyes fixed upon her and Alfred with the same look of suffering and determination that she had seen the night of the wedding; and one day when she was in one of the rooms behind the dais, she heard him pacing to and fro on the raised platform, and saying to himself:—

"It is all for my sins. I must atone—I must atone. It is a warning." His voice was so full of anguish that the queen did not venture to come in upon him then; but her heart fell, for she was sure that some terrible grief was coming to them.

As she sat in sadness and anxiety, the little prince climbed upon her knee, and said:—

"Mother, won't you tell me a story? Hilda used to."

"My fear shall not make my child sad," she thought, and she said:—

"Yes, I will tell you a story, and I will show you a story, too." And she called one of her women.

"Go to the carved oaken chest in the southeast corner of the treasure room, and bring me the manuscript that is wrapped in a blue silken cloth."

The manuscript was brought, and the child watched with the deepest interest while the queen carefully unfolded the silken wrapping. She took out a parchment that was protected by a white leather covering. At the corners were bits of gold filigree work, and in the filigree was traced in enamel, in one corner the head of a lion, in the second that of a calf, in the third a man's face, and in the fourth a flying eagle. In the centre of the cover was a bright red stone that glowed in the light of the great wood fire.

Then the cover was thrown back, and there was a single piece of parchment. It was torn in one place and a little crumpled, and one corner had been scorched in the fire. It was covered with strange signs, most of them in black, but sometimes one was larger than the rest and painted in red, and blue, and green, and gold, in brighter, clearer colors than Alfred had ever seen in silk or in woolen.

"What is it, mother?" he cried. "Did the gods—the old ones—did they give it to you? and did they tell you how to make runes?"

"Hush!" said his mother, looking half fearfully around and making the sign of the cross on the child's forehead. "There are no gods but our own, but there are evil spirits. We must not speak of the old gods. This is a manuscript from Canterbury."

The older sons had come into the room and pressed near to look at the treasure, Ethelbald who had stood beside his father as man by man in the last war with the Danes, Ethelbert, who was but a few years younger, and Ethelred, who was also a tall young man.

"Does it mean anything? asked Ethelred.

"Yes," said his mother. "It tells a part of a story. There must have been much more of it sometime. It was in the convent at Canterbury, and when the Danes burned it—you were a baby, Alfred—the roll was burned; but a thegn saw this piece lying half hidden under a stone where the wind had blown it. The bishop said he might bring it to me, and I had the cover made for it. This is what it says," and she repeated:—

> "Once on a time it happened that we in our vessel
> Ventured to ride o'er the billows, the high-dashing surges.
> Full of danger to us were the paths of the ocean.
> Streams of the sea beat the shores, and loud roared the breakers,
> Fierce Terror rose from the breast of the sea o'er our wave-ship.
> There the Almighty, glorious Creator of all men,
> Was biding his time in the boat. Men trembled at heart,
> Called upon God for compassion, the Lord for his mercy;
> Loud wailed the crowd in the keel. Arose straightway
> The Giver of joy to the angels; the billows were silenced,
> The whelm of the waves and the winds was stilled at his word,
> The sea was calm and the ocean-streams smooth in their limits.
> There was joy in our hearts when under the circle of heaven

"WHAT IS IT, MOTHER?" HE CRIED.

The winds and the waves and the terror of waters, themselves
In fear of the glorious Lord became fearful.
Wherefore the living God—'tis truth that I tell you—
Never forsakes on this earth a man in his trouble,
If only his heart is true and his courage unfailing."

The tall young man listened as eagerly as the child, but when at the end she said:—

"I will give it to any one of you who will learn to repeat it," Alfred spoke first:—

"Will you really give it to the one that will learn it?"

"Yes," said his mother, smiling, "but you are too little. Will you have it, Ethelbald?"

"Songs are good, but fighting is better, so I'll none of it;" and Ethelbert said:—

"Saying poems is for harpers, not for princes;" and Ethelred looked at the red stone on the cover rather longingly, and then at the torn and scorched sheet of parchment, and said:—

"I don't care for pieces of things. Alfred may have it." Alfred was listening eager-eyed.

"Mother, I will learn it, truly I will. The priest will say it to me, and I will learn it. Won't you let me have it?" he pleaded.

"But what would a little boy like you do with it, if you had it?" asked the queen.

"I'd send it to my sister Ethelswitha. Won't you let me take it to the priest?" he begged. The queen yielded, the parchment was rolled up, the silken covering carefully wrapped around it, and a man was sent with the child to find the priest. It was not many days before the priest came with the little prince to the queen and said:—

"My lady, the young prince can say every word of it."

So the boy was put up high on the king's seat in the great hall, and the king and the thegns and the priests and the women of the house all came in to see the wonderful thing. To sing the old ballads, that was nothing; many a man could do that; but to say off something that had come right from a wonderful piece of parchment, that was quite another matter. Some of them were not really sure that there was not some witchcraft about it, and they stood as near the middle of the hall as they could, so that if the evil spirits should come in at either end, they could get out at the other.

Nothing dangerous happened, however. The little boy said the poem, and was praised and petted very much as a child would be to-day for accomplishing some small feat. Then the precious roll was laid on a golden salver, and one of the king's favorite thegns carried it to him, and bending low on one knee, presented it to the little prince.

"And now may I carry it to Ethelswitha?" he asked eagerly.

"It shall be sent to her," said his mother, "and the thegn shall say, 'Your little brother Alfred sends you this with his love'; but Ethelswitha's home is a long way off, and I could not spare my little boy, not even for a single day."

Again there came that strange look into the eyes of the king. He drew Osburga into a room back of the dais, and said:—

"Could you spare your son to save your husband?"

"What do you mean?" Osburga asked. She felt that the mysterious trouble that she had feared was coming upon her.

"Many years ago," said the king, "I wished to become a priest. I gave it up to please my father, because he had no other son; but I vowed to make the pilgrimage to Rome as penance, because I had drawn back after I had put my hand to the plough. My duty to the kingdom, and I am sometimes afraid my love for you,—" and he put his arm tenderly about her,—" has kept me from performing my vow. A warning came. The child that I love best was in the hands of robbers. God interposed with a miracle, and he was saved; but there will not be another miracle. I must not go to

Rome, the kingdom needs me. Shall I lose my soul for my broken vow, or shall I send—?"

"Don't say it, I cannot bear it," begged the queen; but the king laid his finger gently upon her lips, and said:—

"One must give that which he values most. Shall we send Alfred?"

"Not the child," sobbed the queen. "Send the older ones, not the little one. Ethelswitha is gone, and Alfred gone—I cannot bear it."

"One must give what he values most," repeated the king gravely; "and again, it was about Alfred that the warning came. Shall we leave him to be taken from us, or shall we spare him for a little while to save him to us?"

"Let me go with him," pleaded Osburga.

"And leave me alone?" the king answered. "Is it not enough to spare my best-loved son?" and as she looked up in his face, she trembled to see how pale it had become.

"No, I could not leave you," she said. "You are wise, and I am not. You must do what is right, but how can I bear it?"

The next morning there was great excitement, for every one knew that Prince Alfred was going to Rome in the care of Bishop Swithin.

Chapter III.

Alfred Goes to London

It was a long journey to Rome, and almost as much of a distinction for a man to go there as it would be now to visit the planet Mars. There would have been great interest and excitement if the king had been going to make the pilgrimage, but for the little prince, a child of five years, to go was even more thrilling. The priests were very ready that the people should know that it was to atone for his father's deed and to keep his father's vow, that he was going; and many of them sympathized with the little fellow, and thought it very hard that he should have to go over land and sea into that great, unknown, and dangerous world.

Every one loved the king's youngest son, and every one was eager to do something for him before his departure. The spinners and weavers made for him finer linens and softer woolens than they had ever made before; the embroiderers worked most intricate borders of leaves and flowers and circles and squares and scrolls around his tunics. The tunics were made of silk or of the finest woolen, and were of the brightest colors that could be dyed. The bakers were continually sending him tiny loaves of bread made of the finest wheat, and from the brewery would often come little cups of the juice of mulberries sweetened with honey. The tenants who lived farther away could not come near the palace without bringing him nuts or grapes or apples or combs of honey. The smith who had given him his little coat of mail now made him supremely happy by the gift of a tiny sword.

"Did you put a rune on it?" asked Alfred. "You know my father's sword has a rune, and if we meet a Dane, I'm going to cut his head off just like this," and he slashed off the head of a thistle that grew by the forge.

Not only to Alfred himself did the gifts come, but Wynfreda, his nurse, who had taken the place of the thoughtless Hilda, was quite loaded down with all sorts of things for him to use on the way. One of the cooks brought a package of little hard cakes that would keep fresh for a long time, lest he should be hungry on the road and not be able to find anything to eat. Another brought a small bag of salt, because she was sure that in the strange lands over the seas they would not be able to find salt.

The keeper of the dogs quite insisted that he should take at least five or six with him; and one small boy who was a great friend of Alfred's, the son of the king's cup-bearer, came in a procession consisting of himself and a tiny, pink-eyed pig, to offer his pet as a companion for the prince on his journey, the pig all the while expressing his objections in the most energetic squeals. The carpenter brought him a whole armful of wooden toys, and a bow that was polished until it shone. The ends were carved in the shape of a horse's head, and about the horse's neck was a little collar of bronze, and where the collar was fastened, a tiny green jewel shone out.

The queen seemed almost dazed with grief at the approaching separation. She followed him about wherever he went, saying little, but watching every movement. She was continually planning something to make him more comfortable, or to amuse him on his journey. One day she said:—

"Alfred, I am going to give you a gold chain to wear around your neck, and a pretty gold jewel to hang on it. Now what shall the picture be? Shall we have Saint Cuthbert, your own saint?"

"Yes," said Alfred, "and some red roses; but I don't want a helmet. I want to see his face and not pull a chain." The poor queen was somewhat mystified, but she said:—

"I am afraid that Saint Cuthbert did not have any red roses, but he shall have them this time, if you wish."

"And the red rose was on a blue banner," he said. "I want it all blue."

"And what shall his tunic be?" Alfred thought seriously for a minute, and then said:—

"Green."

"It shall be just as you choose to have it," said his mother, "and around the edge shall be written, 'Alfred had me made,' and when you come back from Rome, you shall learn how to read it."

The jewel was made, and the bishop blessed it, and the queen hung it around Alfred's neck, and before many days it was time to start. They were going as directly as they could to the river Thames, and then by boat to London. There they expected to stay for a few days and then to sail for France.

The morning came. The king was going as far as the bank of the river, so he rode first, as he had done at Ethelswitha's wedding, with Alfred on his horse before him. Then came Bishop Swithin, who was to be Alfred's especial guardian, then Wynfreda the nurse and two other women to assist her; and then came a long retinue of armed men, for the king's son must go in state.

When the procession was ready to go, Osburga stood in the door of the palace with Alfred clinging to her. She wore a robe of deep blue richly embroidered with gold. The clasp was of gold filigree set with red stones. Her hair was fastened back with a narrow gold band, and over it and around her neck was

OSBURGA STOOD IN THE DOOR OF THE PALACE
WITH ALFRED CLINGING TO HER.

a white wimple, or veil, of the finest linen. She wore rings and bracelets and chains, more than ever before, even at their greatest banquets. The king looked at her in surprise, and she said:—

"It comes to my heart that I shall never see my son again. He must remember me in my best." Then she lifted the little jewel on his chain, kissed it lightly, and said in a chanting tone and with a strange far-away look:—

"My people had the gift of prophecy. Sometimes to me too it comes, and my thought is full, not of the present, but of the future. Alfred, this is to remind you of me in all the years that are to come; but when it is finally lost to you, do not grieve, for then the hardest days of your life will have passed. Much will even then lie before you, but you will overcome."

Little child as he was, Alfred never forgot those words, and he never forgot his mother as she stood in the palace door in her long blue robe with the glittering jewels, and with one hand extended toward the southwest. Her face was white, and a red spot glowed on either cheek. She kissed him for the last time, and they were gone.

It was not a long ride to the bank of the Thames where it was deep enough for their light vessels. The road was hardly more than a rough track, but it led through the woods, and it was farther from home than Alfred had ever been before; and to so little a boy that was an adventure in itself.

Twice they passed by a little settlement where some noble had built his castle. There they had mead and wine and hot bread and roasted fowls, and the noble came to do homage to his king; and all the children on the place flocked around to gaze shyly at the little boy who sat fearlessly on his father's horse and who was going to the great and wonderful Rome which no one that they knew had ever seen. It was all a marvel, and after the glittering company had passed, they were not really sure that it was not a dream.

But the riders left the little villages and swept on to the banks of the Thames; and there were many boats drawn up to the shore waiting for them. These were light vessels drawing little water, and having but one sail each. On the top of the mast of the boat in which Alfred was to go was an eagle. The prow of the boat was made in the shape of a dragon with a wide-open mouth and great, fiery, red eyes. The stern was made like a dragon's tail. Everything about the boat was bright and shining, and in the middle of the sail was drawn the figure of a white horse in lines of gold. It was very beautiful, but the little prince was disappointed.

"Where are the shields?" he said, "and the spears?"

"The fighting men have them," said his father, a little puzzled.

"But there was a coat of mail on the boat and a blue banner with a red rose, and there was a god. Why isn't it all here?"

"It was one of Hilda's stories," whispered one of the men; and the king said:—

"The true God is with you here, Alfred, and will be on the boat with you, and go all the way, and bring you back to me, if—" but the king could say no more. In a moment he recovered himself and turned to the bishop.

"Bishop Swithin," he said, "I trust to you my beloved son. Care for him as for the apple of your eye. Let not a hair of his head be injured. Let but the least breath of harm come to him, and—"the king's eyes blazed—"I swear to you by all that I hold sacred that, priest and bishop and friend of my father though you are, you shall be hanged like a Dane to the nearest tree." The king sprang upon his great white horse and galloped into the forest, leaving his followers to find their way after him as best they might.

It was little more than one hundred miles to London, and

with wind and current in their favor, it did not need many hours to make the journey. As long as the daylight lasted, Alfred sat at the prow of the boat on a bench made just like his father's on the dais in their own hall. It was covered with a thick, soft cloth of deep red, whose ends were fringed with tiny disks of gold. Bishop Swithin sat beside him, ready to tell him stories and to answer all his questions. On the other side was Wynfreda, his nurse, and behind them were two servants who held a canopy over their heads whenever the sun was too warm.

When the sun went down and it grew chilly, the little prince was warmly wrapped in the softest furs and taken to a sheltered place in the stern, and there he slept as soundly as if in his father's palace, until the sun was well up again, and they had been under way for several hours.

Alfred thought it was a wonderful voyage. To float along hour after hour past woods and meadows and hills that he had never seen before—this of itself was exciting enough, especially when he awoke in the morning and found that it was not all a dream; but besides this, to have the strange city of London before them—it was more than he could imagine, and as for the long journey that would come after London, he could not think of that at all. He had never seen so large a boat before, and he thought it very wonderful that the water was strong enough to hold it up. The bishop tried to explain it to him, and then said:—

"There's another way that water can hold up things. I'll tell you a riddle that a great poet named Cynewulf made a long time ago about water that grew strong."

"Was it before Ethelswitha was married?" asked Alfred.

"Yes, long before. This is the riddle; see if you can guess it.

> "Wonderful deeds by the power alone
> Of one that I watched as he went on his way
> Were done. At his touch the water was bone."

"Can you guess it, Wynfreda?" said Alfred.

Wynfreda said "No," and the bishop said the answer was, "The frost."

There was no time for more riddles, for London was coming into view. They could see a great wall running along the river front, and going back from it up the gentle slope. Here and there was a building tall enough to peer over the top of the wall. There were many boats anchored in front of the city. At the angles of the wall were turrets for the archers, and places of shelter for the sentinels, where they were always watching, and fearing lest the Danes should return, for it was only two years since they had sacked and burned a part of the city.

They came nearer and nearer, and soon the little company of boats left the Thames and went north up the Fleet, which was then a rapid stream, flowing down not far west of the city wall. It was not so easy now, for the strong current was against them; but the rowers were strong, too, and it was not long before they were ready to land the prince and his followers near Lud Gate, a massive door in the great wall that surrounded the city.

There were many people waiting to receive them, the priests from Saint Paul's Church, that was not far away, the commanders of the soldiers who were in the various strongholds, and all the other great men of the city. Some came on foot, and some came on horseback, and a few came in heavy wagons with wide, clumsy wheels; and all of them, no matter how they had come, were eager to do honor to the son of the king. There were women whose eyes were full of tears as they looked at the tiny, blue-eyed, fair-haired child who was so far from his mother, and who was so soon to make the great journey by sea and by land; and there were crowds of boys swarming up the posts and on top of the low-roofed cottages, every one of whom wished that he was the son of the king, and was going to make a wonderful journey.

Some of the ponderous wagons had been brought to convey the prince and his nobles to the palace, for Ethelwulf had a palace in London not far from Saint Paul's Church. These were decorated with bright-colored cloth, and with flowers and green branches. The one in which Alfred was to go had a seat covered with cushions and drapings of bright blue, and built up so high that all the people could see him as he rode past. It made the boys more wildly envious than ever when they saw that he actually wore a coat of mail, and had a real sword hanging down by his side.

They were a little stolid and slow in their thinking, these Englishmen of the ninth century, but there was something in the sight of this little child that appealed to them, and aroused all their loyalty and enthusiasm; and they shouted for Alfred, and for Ethelwulf, and for Bishop Swithin, until they were hoarse, and they followed the wagons until the prince and his retinue had gone into the palace. The bishop stood on the steps a minute, and raised his hand and blessed them. Then he, too, went in, and the tired and excited little child could have the rest that he so much needed.

The palace was a little west of Saint Paul's Church and not far from the river. Around it were fields and woods; and to the westward, beyond the last straggling houses, were pastures and forests and fens and moors and commons and low-lying hills, a beautiful, restful country for tired people to look upon.

The city was made up of small houses, hardly larger than huts, that seemed to have been dropped down anywhere; of convents and churches and fortresses; of rough, tumble-down sheds, and queer little dark shops in which were benches, a table, and some simple arrangements for cooking. Whatever there was to sell was put on a shelf that projected in front of the shop. Far to the east, just within the wall, one could see a fort that was higher and larger than the rest, for there the closest watch must be kept for the enemy, and there, too, if the enemy came, must the hardest fighting be done.

The streets, so far as there were any streets, ran any way, and every building seemed to have been set down without the least regard to any other building. Then too, there were great vacant spaces, and these were gloomy enough, for here were blackened ruins of the city that used to be before the Danes had burned it. Under all this rubbish were fragments of beautiful mosaic pavement that the Romans had made centuries before.

Even then there was enough in London to interest one for a long time, but the first duty of the prince after he was thoroughly rested was to go to Saint Paul's Church with the gifts that his father had sent. The church was at the top of a hill that rose gently from the Thames River. It could hardly have been more than a very simple chapel, built perhaps of stones that may have been part of a heathen temple in the old Roman times, but now the bell rang seven times a day for Christian prayer.

This little church was very rich, for it possessed the bones of Saint Erkenwald, and wonderful were the miracles that they were said to have wrought, and generous were the gifts that pilgrims, nobles, warriors, and kings had laid on his shrine.

Saint Paul's had had a hard struggle to get these relics, for Saint Erkenwald had died when away from London, and both the clergy of Saint Paul's and the monks of Chertsey, whose abbot he had been, contended for the bones. Both parties were very much in earnest. The Londoners seized the bier and held on. The monks protested. A tempest suddenly came upon them, and there they all stood, drenched and dripping, but neither would yield. The river rose, and then they were obliged to stand still, for there was neither bridge nor boat. They might have been standing there yet, had not one of the monks begun to intone the litany; and as he sang, the river sank, and the Londoners crossed with the precious relics, the monks giving up, either because they were satisfied that Providence had settled the question, or because the Londoners were the stronger party, the story does not tell. At any rate, the bones were in Saint Paul's, and there it was that Alfred must go to carry his father's gifts, and to kneel before the shrine of the saint to say the prayers that the bishop had taught him.

And so Alfred and the bishop and the long train of followers set out for the church. The unwieldy wagons moved slowly, but Alfred would have liked to go even more slowly, for there was so much to see that was new to him. There were rough soldiers in leather tunics or in a kind of coat, or jacket, covered with scales that would protect them in battle almost as well as a coat of mail. They had heavy axes and spears and shields. Their beards were long and shaggy. Then there were half-savage men from the country, bringing great, rough carts of timber from the forests, or driving herds of oxen or swine, or carrying rude baskets of vegetables or fruit. They were stout, red-faced men who looked strong and well and ready for a good-natured wrestling match or a downright fight, as the case might be. They wore tunics of the coarsest woolen, and would stop with mouths wide open, and stare with wonder at the sight of the prince and his men with their finely wrought clothes and their jewels and banners.

The royal train went up the hill to the church, and Alfred, taught by the bishop, presented the gifts that his father had sent, seven golden vases fillet to the brim with roughly cut, but bright and shining silver coins. On the side of each one of these vases was a red stone, and below it was the inscription, "Ethelwulf the king sent me."

The service was ended. Alfred had said his prayer before Saint Erkenwald's shrine, and had gazed half fearfully on the bones of the saint. The prince and his followers left the church. There were fragments of the old Roman pavement under their feet.

"See the soldier," said Alfred suddenly, "but he isn't like my father's soldiers." The bishop looked, and there in the pavement was the figure of a soldier done in mosaic.

"That is a Roman soldier," said the bishop, "and we shall start for Rome to-morrow. Look down to the river and you will see the ships that are to take us."

Chapter IV.

Across the Continent

Alfred was not at all pleased with the appearance of the boats that were to take them across the channel and up the Seine River to Paris. Instead of being as bright and shining as they could be made, and ornamented with gold and gorgeous with banners, they were very plain and were painted a dull bluish gray.

"This isn't a pretty boat," said he to one of the noblemen.

"No, my prince," the nobleman replied, "but sometimes it is better not to be seen than to be pretty. The Danes have sharp eyes, and the sun shining on a bit of gold sends a light a long way."

"No danger of Danes in this short run," said another; "we can almost throw a stone across to the fair land of the Franks, and in weather like this, the sea will be as still as a cup of mead."

"That does not stand so very still when it's within your reach," retorted the first.

It seemed needless to think of danger now that the sky was so blue, the shores so green, and everything about them so calm and peaceful. Down the river they went, going by a passage that is now filled up between Thanet and the fields and forests of Kent. And now England was behind them, and—though no one knew it—the hope of England's greatness was at the mercy of the winds and the waves and the frail, open-decked vessel.

"It is the day of all days for the journey of a prince," said Bishop Swithin to the captain.

"It is," said the captain, "but I will not trust it. There's a look to the sky that I don't like, and I half incline to run into harbor at Dover and wait till morning."

"That would mean a day's delay," said the bishop thoughtfully.

"Better delay than danger," said the captain.

"True," said the bishop, "but the king's orders are to make the journey and return as rapidly as the comfort of the prince will permit."

The sky cleared, and the captain against his better judgment steered for the Frankish coast. Hardly were they fairly clear of the land when a strong wind came up from the south, sweeping a heavy mist before it. The boats were separated, but the best seamen of England were in charge of Alfred's vessel, and even then all would have gone well, had not the rudder suddenly given way.

"What will the Danes do to us, if they get us?" asked Alfred. More than one face paled. In the excitement of the storm every one had for the moment forgotten the even more terrible danger that they were in. The wind was driving them directly to the Danish coast, and their boat was rudderless.

"The Danes shall never get you, my prince," said the bishop; and turning aside to a tall thegn, one of the king's greatest warriors, he whispered, pointing to the short sword that hung at his side:—

"You know your duty?"

"I do," said the thegn in a fierce undertone, "but many a Dane shall see the bottom of the ocean before I save the child in that way."

"It would be the king's wish," said the bishop gravely. The thegn made no reply, but under his breath he muttered savagely:—

"These vows!"

The men stood with folded arms. There was nothing for them to do.

The bishop lifted his eyes to heaven and began to intone the litany:—

"Lord, have mercy upon us! From the fury of the Northmen, good Lord deliver us!"

"Good Lord deliver us!" responded the others fervently; but even as they spoke, there was a sudden rift in the fog, and there before them, with a flash of sunshine coming down full upon it, was a Danish fleet.

"They have seen us," said the captain in despair. "They are coming down upon us."

The bishop drew the little prince nearer and wrapped his long cloak about them both.

"Get me a sword while I pray," he said; "and do you pray, my prince, pray for our relief; the prayers of a child go very swiftly."

The sword was brought, but the wind blew them north, and the Danes were coming nearer. The fog had lifted. The English could almost see the fierce, exultant faces of their foes. The bishop did not stir from his place. His head was uplifted, his lips moved, though no sound was heard.

Something had happened to one of the boats of the Danish fleet. It rolled like a log in the trough of the sea. It was sinking, and before the others could come to the rescue, the waters had closed over it.

"It is a miracle," cried one of the sailors, and fell on his knees.

"God's ways are always miracles," said the bishop. "Look!" and behold, the Danes, as superstitious as they were fierce, had fled like so many frightened sea-gulls. They had all sail spread, and the same south wind was quickly sweeping them toward their own coast. The English managed to make one of the benches into a rude substitute for a rudder, and although their voyage to France was slow, they met with no more dangers.

"What made the Danes' boat go down?" asked Alfred, when they were sailing safely up the Seine River.

"We prayed to God, and He made it," said the bishop.

"Would He have made our boat go down if the Danes had prayed to Him?" persisted the child.

"Bishop," said the captain, "my sister's husband knew a man who was in a boat that went down in a minute just as that one did. It was in shallow water, and the tide left the place bare, and they found that the worms had bored the planks through and through. It was soaked with water, but no one guessed what was the matter with it. It minded the rudder and the sail, but it kept going more and more slowly until all of a sudden it went down just like this."

"Even a greater miracle," said the bishop, "if the little creatures of the sea have been called upon to save us. We are grown men, our lives are fast coming to their latter days, but a little child has much before him. Alfred, my prince," he said to the child, who was closely listening, "never forget that God could have saved the Danish boat as easily as ours; and that if He chose to save you, it is because He has work for you to do when you are a man."

Soon they reached Paris, and began their journey through the land of the Franks. It was like a triumphal procession. No one knows how many men were in the company, but there were soldiers enough to make quite a retinue by themselves. Then, too, there were many priests; there were women to assist Wynfreda, or to take her place or that of her special assistants, if anything should befall one of them. Provisions must be carried. Hotels were a comfort of the distant future; kings' courts were rare, and castles and convents where so many could be entertained were not common. They could not trust to buying food along the way; and so there was a long train of packhorses and mules carrying corn and wheat and barley, some of it ground, and some to be ground as they needed it. They had dried and salted meats, beef and pork; they had ale and mead and wine, together with pigment, a heavy, sweet wine, of which they were fond. Cooks and wine-makers were with them, carpenters and smiths and men to care for the horses.

Truly, it was a gorgeous procession. First came half of the soldiers. The nobles among them wore glittering coats of mail, and had spears in their hands, while at their sides hung swords with wooden scabbards covered with leather and bound with bands of bronze. The others wore tunics of bright colors and cloaks, and they had short swords and battle-axes. After these soldiers came the bishop and his priests and the little prince, and Wynfreda with her women, and the men who had charge of the treasure, money to spend and to give away, and gifts for the Pope. Then came a brilliant company of noblemen, more soldiers, and then the long lines of servants with mules and horses laden with rich robes and provisions and fodder for the beasts.

Part of the journey was made over the old Roman roads, and here they could travel as rapidly as was possible for so large a number of people. The Romans used, first, to beat the soil, then to spread layers of flint or pebbles or sand, and then sometimes add a kind of masonry of stones or bricks fastened together with mortar. The roads were raised in the centre, and it seems as if it ought to have been easy to march over them; but there was one great disadvantage, they were as nearly straight as they could be made, and if a hill came in their way, they never went around it, but always directly over it.

Rough roads were not the worst troubles that they had to meet. Streams must be forded, sometimes gentle and winding, flowing softly through green meadows and bordered with bright flowers; but sometimes they were wild and turbulent, and dashed through the mountain gorges with a fierce, dangerous current. At such times, the bishop never trusted Alfred to any one else, but, taking the child on his own saddle-bow, he would carefully pick his way across from rock to rock. Sometimes the stream would be so deep that the horse would have to swim; and then the bishop would have ten men below him ready to rescue the prince, if the force of the current should sweep the horse down stream. After crossing such a torrent as this, the whole company would kneel down on the farther shore, and the bishop would thank God for saving them from death; and then he would chant the "Gloria," and they would go on ready to meet the next danger.

Had the company been smaller, there would have been great fear of robbers, for they had to pass through dense forests where many bands of thieves had made their home.

"The child has been in danger of robbers once," the king had said when they left home, "and please God, he shall not be this time"; and so he had given them an escort three times as large as any one would have thought was necessary.

It was a long journey, and the bishop was glad when they came to a great stone castle where they were to rest a few days; for Alfred was never strong, and the constant travel had been very tiresome for him.

It was quite a climb to the castle, for it was high up on a jutting crag far above the green meadows. It looked gray and stern and forbidding, but its doors were thrown wide open to welcome the great bishop and the little Saxon prince. It would not have been so easy to enter if they had been unwelcome guests; for first they went across a moat by a drawbridge, then through a gate in the thick wall with a strong tower on either hand; then came another moat and bridge and wall, and still another. Overhead was the heavy iron portcullis with its sharp points ready to fall upon them, had they been enemies; but at last they were inside the "keep," the home of the lord of the castle, where he and his family lived and where their richest treasures were kept.

It was a very safe place, and that meant a great deal in those stormy days; but Alfred thought it was the most gloomy house he had ever seen, for the windows were only loopholes, and the rooms were small and cheerless. The greeting was hearty, for the days were rather dull and lonely. There was great rejoicing whenever a wandering minstrel made his way up the mountain, or a priest bound on some distant mission stopped to ask for a night's entertainment. What a welcome there must have been, then, when a bishop and a prince and their long train of followers were seen winding up the narrow, rough way that led to the castle!

Alfred was delighted to find a boy not much older than himself, the youngest son of the lord of the castle. The lord's wife was English, and so little Ekhard could talk English, and the two children had a delightful time. It was all strange and mysterious to Alfred, especially the long underground passage that led far out into the forest; and he thought Ekhard a wonderful boy when he told the story of a time when the castle was attacked, and some of their men had gone through the passageway back of the besiegers and hemmed them in between themselves and the wall.

"Did you kill them?" asked Alfred of this marvelous new friend.

"We dropped hot pitch down on them and drove them into the moat," said Ekhard.

Alfred's eyes were very wide open. He had seen many strange sights since he left his own home, but this was the most amazing of all, for here was a boy not much taller than himself who had seen a real fight. How the little fellow wished that he could be so fortunate!

They sat at the long table at noonday. Part way down the table was the salt-cellar. Above it was the lord with family, his the little prince, the bishop, the priests, and the nobles. Below it were those were those of less rank. There was room for all and entertainment for all. They were still sitting at the table when there was a noise at the gate and the sound of a hunter's horn.

"A man demands speech with my lord," said one of the serving-men.

"The meal hours are sacred," said the lord. "Bid the man enter and share the meal. Afterwards, he may speak.

The man entered, but instead of taking the place that was pointed out to him, he went straight to the lord, bent lightly on one knee before him, and whispered a few words in his ear. The lord sprang to his feet, beckoned to his men at arms, and in a moment all was confusion and uproar. Every man put on a helmet or a coat of mail or whatever he happened to possess in the line of armor, seized a sword or an axe or a spear, and followed his lord.

It was all a mystery to Alfred. Not one word of all the loud talk had he understood. He sat motionless until they had dashed out of the castle gate, and he could hear the steps of their horses going at a breakneck speed down the hill. Then he turned to his friend Ekhard and asked in a frightened whisper:—

"Are the Danes coming?"

"What are Danes?" said Ekhard, a little contemptuously. "This is better than any Danes. Come, and I'll show you," and he seized him by the hand and drew him away to some winding stairs in one of the towers.

"Come, and perhaps we can see the merchants," he said.

"What merchants?" asked Alfred.

"The men that are coming from Italy to our country. They have things to sell."

"Will your father buy some?" asked Alfred.

Ekhard looked as if he thought Alfred a most ignorant young person, if he was a prince, and said:—

"Of course not. Every one that goes by our castle must pay my father. Those men haven't paid, and so he will take their goods."

"Will he kill them?" asked Alfred.

"He will if they fight," said Ekhard. "Come up, and perhaps we can see them." So the two boys, hand in hand, climbed the steep, winding stairs in one of the towers. Through the long, narrow slit in the wall, they could see afar down the valley a little company of men winding slowly along the road. To the right of them, but quite hidden from them by the spur of the mountain, was another company, the lord and his men, hurrying down the steep path to meet the merchants. The traders were soon hidden in the woods, and the lord's men too disappeared, but the two children heard faint shouts and war cries; then all was still.

"I wonder what they'll bring," said Ekhard, and went on talking, half to himself and half to Alfred. "Perhaps there'll be silk and velvet and jewels and furs. The last one had silver and glass and oil. I don't care much about that, but I hope they'll bring some cinnamon and nutmeg and wine and dried fruits."

"Why won't your father let people go by his house?" said Alfred. "My father does."

"Why, because he's the lord, and they have to pay him," said Ekhard; "but we can't see any more. Let's go down and meet them."

It seemed a long time to the impatient children before the lord and his men came up the hill. Their march was slow, for the men were on foot, and every horse was laden with booty. There were rolls of silk and fine woolen, precious stones and carved ivory, a package of stained glass for the windows of some church, and what pleased Ekhard most, a great quantity of cinnamon and cloves and figs and dates.

"That's a good load," said he to Alfred; but Alfred was thinking, and thinking very earnestly for so little a boy. He looked at the bishop, but the bishop was at the farther end of the long room. Then he went to Wynfreda.

"Didn't those things belong to the merchants?" he asked.

"Yes," said Wynfreda.

"My father wouldn't take them away," said he. "I won't when I am a man."

The hardest part of their journey was still before them, for the Alps lay between them and Rome. They were going over the Mount Cenis Pass. There were great forests of pine and fir through which they must make their way. There were bald ridges of jagged rock and deep gorges. Sometimes the road led over dreary slopes. or through dismal ravines, or over fields of snow. Sometimes it was only a tiny thread of a path winding along the edge of a precipice. The bishop looked worn and anxious, but Alfred thought it was all a delightful series of adventures. He clapped his hands with pleasure when he was carefully wrapped in an oxhide and drawn over the snow; and when they came to ledges so dizzy that the horses and mules had to be lowered with ropes to a place where there was surer footing, he thought this was almost as good as seeing a real battle, and wished he could tell Ekhard about it.

The journey was not all danger and no pleasure, not even the passage over the Alps, for a little lower down the flowers were brighter and more beautiful than Alfred had ever seen before. All along the roadside were columbines and geraniums. Harebells clung to every little over-hanging rock. Violets were in the shady nooks of the forest. The lady's-slipper was there, and down in the warm, sunny meadows below them were beds of pinks. At the edge of the snow above them was the edelweiss. It was all very beautiful, and when they came to their first bed of brilliant Alpine roses, Alfred fairly shouted with delight.

"Can't I send some to my mother?" he begged, but the bishop smiled and said:—

"You shall take her something better than roses. There are wonderful things in Rome, and you shall choose among them."

And so they went on to Rome; but outside the city three men on horseback met them.

"Is this the train of the noble prince, Alfred of England?" said they.

"It is," said the bishop.

"Then is there a message from King Ethelwulf. The bearer came at the risk of his life. He is ill, and he begs that you will come to him, for the king's business brooks no delay."

Chapter V.

"My Pope"

"The king's business brooks no delay," said the bishop to himself, as with the three men for guides he rode through the streets of the city to the abiding place of the king's messenger.

"A greeting to you, Wulfric," said the bishop, "bold and trusty thegn of my king that I know you to be. What brings you into so sad a plight?" for the thegn lay on his bed and was evidently in great distress. Drops of perspiration stood on his forehead, and his face was drawn with suffering.

"Think not of me," said the thegn. "Do not lose a moment. I fear that it is already too late. Osburga, the wife of our king, is dying. Take the prince to her. With that message am I sent."

"But what has come to the queen?" asked the bishop. "Is it the grief from the parting?"

"Yes," said the thegn. "She pined for the prince, and faded so rapidly that the king sent me to intercept you and give his command that you bring back the child to his mother."

"Where is your guard?" asked the bishop. "You are alone?"

"I came alone," answered the thegn. "My mother was one of the Franks. I know the language of the peoples through whose lands one must pass. I told the king that I could make my way faster if I was alone, that I knew footpaths and secret ways through the mountains where one man might go, but not an armed troop."

"And to bring a child to his mother, you have come alone where we scarcely ventured with a great guard of armed men?"

"It was the will of the king," said the thegn simply, "and all would have been well, had I not—and I was but a few miles from your road—if I had only not been taken by robbers, I should have met you; but that was many days ago. They held me for a ransom. I begged for only a few hours to meet you and give you my message, but they laughed me to scorn. I could not wait for the ransom; the king's business brooks no delay. I escaped. They caught me and tortured me and left me for dead. I made my way here, I know not how, and our own Saxons in Rome have cared for me most tenderly. I shall die, but tell my king that I was faithful to my trust."

The bishop's eyes were full. He bent low and kissed the thegn's hand.

"My bishop!" the suffering man gasped in protest.

"To-morrow I shall come to you again," said the bishop. "The prince cannot travel without rest. The king must not lose both wife and child."

Scarcely was the bishop again on the street when there was a great clattering of hoofs. He turned, and there was a company of riders with the familiar Saxon dress and weapons. The bishop's heart sank.

"If it was well with her," he thought, "there would be no message."

The foremost of the riders dismounted, bowed himself low before his bishop, and presented a bit of parchment in a strong leather case. It read:—

"Ethelwulf the king sends greeting to Swithin his bishop, and bids him know that Osburga, the wife of the king, is dead; and that it is the king's will that Alfred the prince tarry in Rome until the king come to him."

The bishop was a good man of business as well as a prelate, and it was but a short time before the prince was comfortably established for a longer stay than they had planned. Not until he had had many days of rest did the bishop give him the message from his father. Then very tenderly he told him that when he went home his mother would not be there to meet him.

"But I was going to carry her the prettiest gift in Rome," said he, his great blue eyes filling with tears, "and now she won't have it."

"You can pray for her," said the bishop, taking the child into his arms, "and that is better than any gift in all Rome."

"But I wanted to carry her something," said the little boy, and in spite of all the tender care and sympathy of the bishop and Wynfreda, the little Saxon prince was that night the saddest, loneliest child in Rome.

The Saxons were nominally guests of the Pope, Leo IV, and very soon came the first interview with him. Leo was much pleased with the little boy who quietly did just what he was told to in the formal ceremony of his reception; and he was far more pleased when the child, after a long look straight into his eyes, came up to him fearlessly and laid his little hand in that of Pope.

"That is a child with the soul of a prince," said the Pope. "Some day he will be a king, it needs no prophet to foretell that there will turbulent days in that stormy, harassed land of the Saxons. Perhaps he will not wear his crown until long after I am gone, but no hand save mine shall anoint him with the holy oil." And so holy oil was brought, for Leo was not a man of delays and postponements, and the child was anointed and blessed. Then the Pope said, touching the jewel that hung at Alfred's throat:—

"And what is this? Is it a relic?"

"It is my Saint Cuthbert," said the boy. "My mother gave it to

THEN THE POPE SAID... "AND WHAT IS THIS? IS IT A RELIC?"

me, and I was going to carry her the prettiest thing in all Rome; but now I can't, because she is dead." The Pope laid his hand tenderly on the child's head.

"The Saxon prince comes nearer to my heart than any other child has ever done," he said. "He has his sponsors in baptism, but he shall have one more. I hereby adopt him as my own spiritual son. I give him the blessing of the Father of the Church, and I give him the kiss of the tired old warrior whose heart he has warmed with his childish trust," and the Pope bent down and kissed the boy gently on the forehead.

Very little of this speech had Alfred understood, for it had all been in Latin, but he had many questions to ask about it, and Bishop Swithin tried to make him comprehend the meaning of the ceremony. The next morning he asked to be taken again to see "my Pope," as he persisted in calling the warrior pontiff, but a council of bishops was to be held in Rome, and it was quite a long time before the Pope could be free to see his little friend.

Month after month passed on, and Ethelwulf did not come. He had hoped to start at once, but one trouble after another in his kingdom prevented him from leaving it. Meanwhile there was much to see in this great city of Rome, the very centre of art and learning, and the months passed swiftly. Soon after their arrival, Alfred had noticed some men heavily chained who were working on the rebuilding of the fortifications.

"My father's men do not wear chains," he said. "Why do these men?"

The bishop explained to him that just as the Danes troubled England, so the Saracens, a people who lived across the sea, had troubled Rome.

"They tore down the holy churches of Saint Peter and Saint Paul," he said, "and robbed them. The sacred pictures they ran through with their knives. The precious stones were torn from the altar, and the golden images and consecrated dishes were carried away to serve in the land of the heathen."

"When the Danes came, my father and Ethelbald fought them and drove them away," said Alfred. "Why didn't my Pope drive them away?"

"He was not Pope then," said the bishop, "but just as soon as he became Pope, and knew that they were coming again, he built those two great towers that you can see from the window, one on each bank of the Tiber, and he stretched a heavy iron chain between them, so that the fleet of the heathen Saracens could not come up the river. Then he repaired the walls and put up new watch-towers. Before long the Saracen fleet came, and the Pope's fleet went out to meet them, and there was a great fight."

"We didn't fight when we saw the Danes," said Alfred.

"No," said the bishop. "We had prayed to God, and He had sent the little worms of the sea to aid us. The Pope's people, too, had prayed, and while they were fighting, a strong wind arose, and the boats of the heathen were separated. Some of them were dashed on the rocks, and all the men were drowned; and some of the men in the other boats were cast away on little islands where there was nothing to eat, and they starved to death; and many were driven on this coast and were taken prisoners, and they are the men whom you saw in chains. They tried to overthrow the Holy City, and now it is their strength that is being used to rebuild it and to fortify it so that no one shall ever be able to come against it again."

"Is it where the high walls are that they are building?" asked Alfred.

"Yes," said the bishop, "in the Vatican quarter. They call it the Leonine City, because the name of your Pope is Leo. He has consecrated it to heaven so that no wicked Saracens can ever prevail against it. A little while before we came, he walked around the wall with many bishops and all the Roman clergy, and sprinkled it with holy water. They were barefooted and had ashes on their heads. At each of the three gates they stopped and prayed that heaven would bless the city, and save it from the heathen men who hated it. Then, because they wished everybody in Rome to be as happy as they were, they gave away great sums of money to the people that were there. To-morrow you shall go again to see the new church of Saint Peter that is within the high walls."

But when the next day came, a messenger arrived from King Ethelwulf, bidding Swithin return at once to England. The king was sad from the loss of his wife, and longed to see his youngest and best-beloved son. Had he read the will of heaven aright, he wondered? Ought he to have sent the child to Rome to keep his father's vow, even to save the boy from fancied danger? Was the death of his wife a punishment for his neglect of duty? He was anxious and restless. He would send for Swithin and the child to return to England, and he would be separated no more from his son, but would take Alfred with him and make his pilgrimage to Rome even at this late day; and so it was, that instead of going to Saint Peter's Church, Alfred started on the long journey across the mountains. The Pope had for many weeks been too ill to see him, so that his little friend could give him no farewell.

It was a lonely time. The bishop was troubled. He was a brave man, and a man of resources, but the care of a delicate child on a second long and dangerous journey was no light matter, and the great responsibilities that awaited his arrival in England were enough to make the most self-reliant man serious. He was much relieved when, before they had travelled many hours, a second messenger from the king met him.

"It is better," said the king, "for me to wait than for the prince to make the journey twice. I bid you leave him in a place of safety to await my coming, and do you make all haste to England."

And so Alfred was left with Wynfreda and a strong guard of nobles, to wait for his father and to make a still longer visit in Rome.

Swithin pushed on to England, and found King Ethelwulf eagerly awaiting his arrival.

"My wife is gone, my child is across the sea and the land," said he sadly. "I have done my best. The country is no longer troubled by the Danish heathen. Surely now I may give up the kingdom to younger hands, and spend my last years in Rome, as did two of my ancestors."

This was what Swithin had feared. He must look for the good of the church rather than for the happiness of the king. If Ethelwulf gave up his kingdom, it would go into the hands of Ethelbald, who was strong, self-willed, and the only one of the king's sons whom the bishop had never been able to influence. Ethelbald cared nothing for the church, and under him it would have neither gifts nor protection. Swithin thought rapidly. Only the most perfect frankness would influence this man, who, hesitating and sometimes weak as he was in matters relating to the government of his kingdom, was never weak or hesitating in matters relating to truth.

"My king," he said, "the kingdom is free from the enemy, but is the church free from her foes? The church in Rome is cared for and protected, but does not the church in England still need your care? Will you spend your life in Rome that the church may give to you? or will you remain in England that you may give to the church? I counsel that you make the pilgrimage, and so free your soul from the shadow of a vow, and then return to aid the church in the country where God has placed you, and among the duties that he has laid upon you."

As the bishop counseled, so it was. In the presence of Swithin and another bishop, Ethelwulf signed a charter freeing one-tenth of his lands from royal tribute and devoting them to the service of the church, and set out eagerly for Rome. The king of the Franks received him with the greatest honors, and would have gladly kept his royal guest for months, but Ethelwulf was too anxious to reach Rome and to meet his favorite son again to be willing to delay. He pressed on, and the Frankish king could do nothing more than to give him his royal escort to the boundary of the kingdom.

Alfred had come a day's journey to meet him, and now a second time the little prince entered Rome, and this time with his father.

"I want to show you my Pope," were the little boy's first words as they entered the city; but the city was draped with black, for the warrior Pope who had defended it so bravely and wisely against its enemies was dead, and every one mourned for him, none more sincerely than the little Saxon boy and his father.

A few days later, a priest was quietly praying in his church, when he was interrupted by the news that he had been chosen as the successor of Leo IV. He begged with tears to be released.

"The charge is too much for me," he said. "I am not equal to it. I am not worthy," but in spite of all his protests, he was carried to the Lateran Church and set on the throne; and so it was that Ethelwulf and his son became guests of Benedict III instead of Alfred's friend, Leo IV.

Ethelwulf's generosity, if nothing more, would have made him a most welcome visitor, for he brought to the Pope gifts that were indeed worthy of a king. There was a crown of pure gold, four pounds in weight, a sword with golden hilt, dishes of gold and of silver set with jewels, many priestly vestments, among them costly stoles with borders of gold and purple, and robes of white samite heavily embroidered with gold and with jewels.

One whole year he spent in Rome, and there seemed to be no limit to his benefactions. He gave gold and silver to Saint Peter's Church, and made generous presents to both clergy and nobles and to the common people. Accustomed as the Romans were to the lavishness of royal pilgrims and to their presence in the Roman streets, these former visitors were quite outshone by this sovereign of a far-away country, who could not speak their language, and whose very name they could not pronounce.

There had been in Rome for many years a school to educate Saxon priests, but this had been burned. Ethelwulf rebuilt it and endowed it. He was not satisfied with his present gifts, but promised one hundred marks a year to the Pope, and the same sum to the church of Saint Peter, and also to Saint Paul's, to provide oil for the lamps for Easter even and Easter morning.

This church of Saint Peter was the jewel of Rome. Protected by the mighty walls of the Leonine City, forty feet in height, it was a treasure-house of all that was rich and costly. Leo had covered the altar with plates of gold, flashing and flaming with precious stones. A silver crucifix was set with amethysts and diamonds, and a golden cross with pearls, opals, and emeralds. There were priceless vases and censers and chalices set with many jewels. There were lamps hung by silver chains ending in golden balls, and there were reading desks of wrought silver. Heavy tapestry in dim, rich colors hung at the doors and on the columns. The priests had vestments of silk and of purple velvet embroidered with gold thread and blazing with precious stones. Ethelwulf, as well as Alfred, had been accustomed to nothing more grand than the English cathedral at Winchester, and this, with the river flowing gently down the valley, the woods all around the little town, and the green hills looking down upon it, seemed like a quiet country chapel in comparison with the magnificence of Saint Peter's in its rich setting of the great Roman city with its towers and churches and monasteries, and its hills crowned with lordly castles.

It was a happy year for the king. He was free from the cares of a turbulent kingdom, which had always been irksome to him. He could spend long hours at his prayers in the churches richly adorned with the gifts of believers, until he could almost fancy that he had at last entered upon the convent life for which he had longed, and forget that he must ever again take up the duties of his kingdom.

But Bishop Swithin was sending him messages that the country needed its king, and at last he reluctantly turned his steps northward to find himself at the Frankish court. Its glitter and its gayeties were at first almost a shock to his highly wrought feelings; but after a little, the very contrast aroused and interested him, and yielding to the urgent invitation of Charles the Bald, he lingered month after month. Next to Rome, this Frankish capital, with the influence of Charlemagne still upon it, was the centre of all culture and the home of all magnificence.

Alfred had hoped to find a little boy like Ekhard, but he forgot his disappointment when he met the king's eldest daughter. She was just about the age that Ethelswitha had been at her marriage. The little brother had missed his sister sorely, and he could almost fancy in meeting Judith that Ethelswitha had come back to him, only she had been quiet and gentle, while this Judith was never twice the same. Sometimes she would put on all the airs of a great lady and insist upon his imitating the manners of some dignified courtier, and then in the midst of all the mock formality, she would suddenly seize his hand, gather up her long skirts, and away they would run down the corridors in a merry race. Even more wonderful than Ekhard, the boy that had seen a battle, was this fascinating Judith, always changing, never twice in the same mood, but always kind to him.

While Alfred was so happy, his father was troubled, for he knew in the bottom of his heart that he ought to return to his kingdom. The Danes had spent the winter on the island of Sheppey, and the country needed its king. Still he delayed to leave this stately court, many of whose ways were so congenial to him. Into the midst of his meditating came one day his little son, who had evidently been meditating too in his small way. He began:—

"Father, I like Judith."

"Yes," said the king, rather absently, "she seems to be a merry, agreeable young girl."

"Shall we go home to Wessex again after we have been here longer?" The king started; the child seemed to have read his thoughts.

"Yes," he said slowly.

"Then can't Judith go too? Will you ask her father?"

Like most people who waver and hesitate over lesser affairs, Ethelwulf often decided weighty matters with a rather astonishing haste. Ever since he left England he had dreaded to return to the lonely palace from which he had fled. Would it not be easier to return if he could take with him this merry, lighthearted young girl? Before nightfall he had asked the Frankish king for the hand of his daughter in marriage.

Chapter VI.

Ethelbald's Revolt

King Charles had no objections to bring forward. Offers of marriage from sovereigns were rare. England was in a troubled state, but in no worse condition than his own country. The consent of the girl herself was hardly asked, but at any rate, she showed no opposition. The betrothal was announced, and in three months the wedding was celebrated with all the pomp and splendor that even the Frankish court could command.

One thing the father of the bride had insisted upon—that she should be crowned queen of the Saxons. At that Ethelwulf hesitated. Long before this time the West Saxons had been aroused to wrathful indignation by the ill conduct of the wicked Queen Eadburga, and ever since the first year of the reign of King Egbert, father of Ethelwulf, it had been a law among them that no woman should be crowned. The royal consort was called the king's wife, not the queen, and she was forbidden to sit beside her husband on the royal seat. Then he remembered that Osburga had often been addressed as queen, and apparently no resentment had been aroused, and with his natural carelessness of ills that were in the future, he suffered the archbishop of Rheims to place the crown of the West Saxons on the head of Judith.

Alfred was very happy when he was told that Judith was to go home with him, but the matter of the marriage was something of a mystery, and when Wynfreda asked him:—

"Have you kissed your new mother?" and led him up to Judith, he said gravely:—

"Judith is my sister; she's my sister for always, and she says she won't ever go away from me as Ethelswitha did;" and Judith, the careless, trivial girl, who had willingly married a man four times her age that she might become a queen, forgot her new crown and her coronation robes, and gave her little stepson a kiss of genuine affection that promised well for her kindness to him, whatever her behavior to others might be.

The wedding festivities were hardly over when a message came to Ethelwulf from his faithful bishop. It was but these few words:—

"O king, if you would still have a kingdom, return to it." Judith, who had the curiosity of a child to see her new domain and an ambition which made her wiser than the king, urged their departure, and they set sail for England.

Some time before this, there had been a long conversation between Ethelbald and Alstan, the soldier bishop of Sherborne, who thirty years before had marched with Ethelwulf at the head of the army into Kent. It was perhaps chiefly owing to Alstan's good advice that Ethelwulf had been able to govern Kent in such a manner as to satisfy his father that he would be able to rule the West Saxons; and all through his reign, while he sought Swithin in religious matters, it was to Alstan that he turned with all questions of practical government. It is this old friend and adviser of the king who now sits in the council chamber of Ethelbald, his keen gray eyes bent upon the ground.

Ethelbald looked at him rather impatiently. Then he spoke:—

"Have you anything to say?"

"Much," said the bishop curtly. "You tell me that you, the eldest son of our king, you who have been trusted with the kingdom during his absence on a holy pilgrimage—"

"And haven't I ruled it well?" broke in Ethelbald, as the bishop hesitated for a moment.

"You have ruled your father's people well; but now you would be faithless to your trust, you would even by force of arms hold the kingdom regardless of the duty that you owe to your father and king."

"That's the speech of a priest," sneered Ethelbald; "that comes from the cloister and the cowl, and not from the man who has marched at the head of an army. I hold this kingdom. I have ruled it well. It is my birthright. One Judith made trouble enough in the land of the Franks. It is a fated name, and shall it come into this land to work misery and overthrow for us too? Shall I be thrust out of my birthright by children of this second marriage?"

"That could hardly be," said the bishop. "The church—"

"Yes, the church would do as it did in the Frankish land," said Ethelbald. "It would stand by the children of the second marriage. Lands that had even been already assigned to the older sons were taken back to make a patrimony for the child of the interloper, and the church had no word of protest."

"Your brothers—" began the bishop, but Ethelbald interrupted.

"Yes, I know all that. You would say that my brothers would stand by me. I know, too, that I am strongest of them all. Ethelbert and Ethelred would nod when I nodded. Alfred is a child. My father always loved him best. If it was not too deep a scheme for my father to have in hand, I should think that all this sending the boy to Rome and this foolishness of the anointing was meant to give him a hold on the kingdom before us who are older."

"I have it from those who were present that it was the Pope's own thought," said the bishop.

"I've nothing against the child," said Ethelbald, his voice softening a little in spite of himself, "and, moreover, if my father were to die to-night, I would take the boy, if I had to fight for him, and I would treat him well, and have him taught what a prince ought to know."

"To be false to his father?" said the bishop, looking fixedly into the young man's eyes.

"I tell you there's no falseness about it. I have in my hands what ought to come to me in a few years at most; and to prevent its being stolen from me I hold on to it. I'll tell you more, bishop. Three days ago, in the forest of Selwood, some forty people met. There were nobles, and there were even some of your own churchmen. Do you want to know what they did? I will tell you. Every man there, be he noble or priest, every man laid his hand on mine and swore by the cross at the hilt of my sword that he would stand by me in my rights. Take that and think upon it; and I'll tell you one thing more, I shall be at the head of this kingdom, and if you and your church want any care or protection from me in the days to come, do you stand by me now," and he strode away, leaving his guest to make his way out as best he might.

The bishop rode slowly away. The shadows began to lengthen; still he rode on, meditating, trying to think what was best to be done. He well knew the disposition of Ethelwulf, that with peace and freedom from care, he would be satisfied. He would give his life to prayer and penance. The loss of his kingdom might be to the gain of his soul. Then it was true that Ethelbald's rule in these months of his regency had been just, though severe. He had ruled by fear rather than with his father's gentle sway, but he had ruled justly and firmly. Was it not true that a king who had left his kingdom, who had taken the money needed in his own land and wasted it in Rome—but here the bishop checked his thought, crossed himself, and said:—

"He did not need to dally in the Frankish court. Save for that, all might have been well. Then too, he, the king, has broken the law of his kingdom. Since the days of the wicked woman whose name may not be spoken among us, no woman may be crowned queen of the West Saxons. There is reason—"

"If your reverence would only turn the horse a bit away from the tuft of grass, my setting of eggs would not be spoiled," said a shrill voice in a tone half-way between scolding and entreating; but it was too late. The bishop's horse had prevented a whole nestful of embryo chickens from ever taking their proper place in the world.

The bishop aroused himself. Where was he? He had wandered far from his road, and now it was late in the afternoon. He made his apologies to the woman who owned the eggs, and added weight to his words by the gift of a silver penny. She was volubly grateful, but he hardly heard her thanks, for he was thinking:—

"It is the hand of some saint that has led me out of my way. This hut is on the road to Winchester." He turned to the woman.

"Have you a stout son whom you could send to Sherborne to say that I am gone to Winchester?" he asked, for he had come to a sudden conclusion; he would go to Winchester and discuss this matter with Swithin; for warrior as he was, Alstan had much respect, even in worldly matters, for the unworldly simplicity of thought of his brother bishop.

It was late in the night when he reached Winchester. Swithin was keeping a vigil before the altar. With almost a touch of impatience, Alstan broke in upon his devotions:—

"It is good to pray, but the time has come when we must think and perhaps fight." Then he told him of his interview with Ethelbald.

"I feared," said Swithin, "that it would come to this, and ten days ago I sent a swift messenger to Ethelwulf. I cannot think that the king will delay longer. But come away to a place where we can be free from interruption, and discuss what is best to do for the church in this troublous time."

"We must plan not only for the good of the church," said the bishop who had been at the head of an army. "The weight of the best good of the kingdom and of the king is thrown upon us."

While this conversation was going on, Ethelwulf, Judith, and Alfred, and their train of warriors and nobles were on their way to England. Their retinue was even longer and more brilliant than it had been at Ethelwulf's first coming, for large numbers of the Frankish nobles followed them to the sea to do honor to the young princess and her royal husband.

The king was silent and troubled; he dreaded the responsibilities of the kingdom, and wished only for quiet and peace, and freedom from the cares that were so wearisome to him. Judith and Alfred were in high spirits, behaving like the two children that they were, until Judith would suddenly remember that she was queen of the West Saxons, and would demand that Alfred should show her the reverence due to a queen. Then Alfred would doff his little cap, and bending low before her with his fair hair blowing in the wind, would repeat the words that she had taught him:—

"Fair lady, princess of the Franks and queen of the West Saxons, I do faithfully avow my—" but rarely would she allow him to go even so far, before the queen in her would vanish, and again they were two children playing together.

When they landed, there was a large company assembled to greet them. The rich waved banners, and the poor waved branches of oak or of evergreen. There were harps and horns and tabors and drums and trumpets; and best of all, there were great shouts of welcome. Alstan had thought it wiser to remain in Wes-

THEN ALFRED WOULD DOFF HIS LITTLE CAP, AND ... WOULD REPEAT THE WORDS SHE HAD TAUGHT HIM.

sex to delay, if he could not prevent, any uprising of the party of Ethelbald; but Swithin was the first to greet the king as he stepped from the boat.

"Welcome, most royal king and master," said the bishop.

"Greeting to you, the beloved master and teacher of the king," said Ethelwulf.

The bishop bowed low before Judith and said:—

"A fitting welcome to the fair princess of the land of the Franks, the wife of our king."

"I am the queen of the West Saxons," said Judith, drawing herself up proudly.

The bishop's face paled. "May I beg in all humbleness—" he began, but Judith turned haughtily away.

Alfred would wait no longer to greet his old friend, and he whispered in the bishop's ear:—

"It's my Judith. She's going to be my sister and stay with me always."

Horses were in waiting, and the royal party rode to the king's palace. The shouts of welcome continued, and the long lines of people that followed them still waved their banners and their green branches; but Swithin was watching keenly, and here and there in the crowd he saw lips firmly set or a look of dull anger, or a stern and fixed gaze bent sullenly upon the king and his new wife, and once he heard a voice that said:—

"That gold would have rebuilt our city and protected us from the heathen;" and another responded:—

"It is not so hard to find a king that will keep the laws. One need not go far."

After the king had withdrawn into the palace, these speeches became more frequent. The bishop fancied that he could trace men going about in the crowd with a word to this man and to that. He fancied that brows became more lowering, and that an expression of dull, slow anger was spreading over many faces. He turned sadly toward the palace. A man mounted on a swift horse drew rein suddenly, peered into the bishop's face, flung himself from his horse, and said:—

"Bishop Swithin, the friends of Ethelbald and those that still remain loyal to the king are to meet in Saint Paul's to-morrow directly after the service."

And so, after Ethelwulf had offered up in the cathedral his thanks for his safe return, there was a meeting of men loyal to their king and men eager to keep Ethelbald on the throne. In spite of all the boasts of Ethelbald, he dared not defy the authority of the church; and the bishops, realizing that the complaint of the West Saxons had just cause, dared not defy the increasing power of Ethelbald. The end of it all was that the two bishops were sent to announce to Ethelwulf the decision of the council, that Wessex at least must remain in the hands of Ethelbald.

Swithin's eyes were fixed upon the king as Alstan told him that it was only by flame and bloodshed that he could hope to remain ruler of the West Saxons. Even the two bishops who had known Ethelwulf from his childhood were not prepared for what followed, for the king sank upon his knees and said:—

"I thank Thee that my prayer is answered, and that I may be free from the worldly anxieties of the ruler of a kingdom;" but Judith, who had insisted upon being present and sitting on the royal seat beside the king, stamped her foot in an almost childish rage and cried out:—

"But I am a queen, and I will not give up my kingdom. Fight! Kill those stupid men who would dare to hold it from me," and the child-queen burst into tears. Alfred had slipped in unnoticed.

"Don't cry, Judith," he pleaded. "If my brother Ethelbald has a kingdom, I'll ask him to let you be queen."

Ethelwulf was only too ready to compromise; indeed, he would have been glad to be rid of the kingdom altogether. It was settled that Ethelbald should remain ruler of the West Saxons, and that Ethelwulf should rule over Kent and the lands adjoining.

"And shall I be queen of Kent?" asked Judith, to whom the wide territories of Wessex and the rather scanty boundaries of the eastern districts were only a name.

The people of Kent had been ruled over by Ethelwulf in his youth, and they remembered and loved the gentle, kind-hearted king, and welcomed him most sincerely. They had no law against the king's wife being called the queen, so that for the time being Judith's ambition was satisfied. The king was even happier than he would have been in Rome, for now that he was really performing the duties of a sovereign, though on so small a scale as not to be wearisome, he had no haunting thoughts that he was neglecting the work that it belonged to him to do.

Never did king lose his kingdom so joyfully. He was free for long hours in the church. He could hear as much singing of psalms as he chose, and to the Anglo-Saxon taste, that was an almost unlimited amount. The singing of psalms in generous measure was an important part, not only of the church service, but also of private devotions. If a man was bound to fast for a day, he might instead sing the one hundred and nineteenth psalm six times. In return for Ethelwulf's gift of lands on his departure for Rome, the churches at Winchester and Sherborne were bound to sing fifty psalms every week "on the day of Mercury, that is Wednesday," for the good of the king's soul. Nor was this singing unaccompanied, for, if we may trust the old records, "Whole pipes of copper being winded by bellows, and furnished with proper stops and keys, sent forth a most loud and ravishing music that was heard at a great distance."

Ethelwulf was in a dream of happiness. He forgot that either Judith or Alfred had any claims upon him, and they were left to amuse each other as best they might. Alfred was fond of telling Judith of his brothers, especially of Ethelbald, who had so impressed his imagination because he was the only one of them that had seen a real battle.

One day there was a great winding of horns and a trampling of horses' feet on the road that led to the royal palace in Kent.

"It is the horn of King Ethelbald of the West Saxons," was whispered half timidly about the palace. Ethelwulf was at church, but Judith had quickly arrayed herself in her richest robes and had taken her place on the royal seat when Ethelbald was ushered in.

A tall man of large frame, with dark complexion and keen, dark eyes bowed half mockingly before her; then, after a quick glance at her face, he bent on one knee to kiss her hand, and said:—

"Ethelbald, king of the West Saxons, bows before the beautiful queen of the kingdom of Kent—and, by my faith, I never saw so fair a face," he added boldly. Judith manifested no anger at the impertinent familiarity. The boldness of Ethelbald was more to her taste than the quiet courtesy of Ethelwulf, and when he said, "Such beauty as this should rule over a wider realm than the narrow limits of Kent and Surrey, it would best grace a queen of the West Saxons, but there is no other face like it," even then she was not angry, but pleased that the stern Ethelbald had yielded so easily to her charms.

"Ethelbald likes Judith," said Alfred to his father. "He told her she ought to be queen of the West Saxons, but you won't let her go, will you?"

"No," said the king, absently; and added: "There is to be a course of one hundred psalms chanted to-morrow morning in the church for the welfare of the country. It may some day be deserted by men and beasts, and while we may, it is fitting that we should offer up sacrifices for it and for the many good men that have given their lives in its service. Will you bring Alfred to the church, Judith?"

"Yes," said Judith as absently, for her thoughts were far away with the man who had not only stolen his father's kingdom, but who, as he rode away, had dared to toss a kiss to the bride of his rightful king.

Chapter VII.

Queen Judith

The next two years were the happiest period of Ethelwulf's life since his coronation. The people of Kent had welcomed him and had found no fault with his marriage. His delight in being free to give his time to the church was intensified by the happiness of those around him. He had all the pleasures of a king and almost none of the responsibilities. He could occupy himself in planning generous gifts to the church and in signing charters to enrich some monastery. He could entertain holy pilgrims and rejoice in their promises that many prayers should be offered for the benefit of his soul. He need not take the king's place at the head of the army, for Ethelbald's energetic measures and his reputation, which had spread even to Denmark, had given the land a respite from her tormentors. At his son's usurpation of the kingdom, Ethelwulf felt not the slightest indignation. He looked upon it rather as a providential event by which he was enabled to give his life to what would bring him most enjoyment and most profit; and he greeted Ethelbald with the utmost cordiality, and even invited him to listen to a special course of psalms to be sung for his benefit when the king of the West Saxons came to Kent with some paper that he thought his father's signature might make more binding on the priests, or on those nobles who, though silent for fear of Ethelbald's strong hand, were still loyal to the rightful king.

Judith had been free to introduce into the court whatever she chose of form and ceremony. The people of Kent were as fascinated as Alfred with the sparkling beauty of their queen and her alternate merriment and stateliness, and criticised nothing that she did. Some of them felt that it was an honor to be allied with the Frankish kingdom; and others remembered that Ethelwulf's bride had been won while he was on his return from a holy pilgrimage, and even fancied that this gave an additional shade of sacredness to the marriage. Osburga had been little known in Kent, so comparisons were never made between her unvarying gentleness and Judith's occasional waywardness. Ethelwulf gladly left much of the royal power in her hands. When the thegns came to consult the king, it was often the fair Judith who met them, heard their story, and decided matters as best suited her whim for the moment. The thegns never knew what to expect from her, but they were sure that she would let no man leave her dissatisfied with her treatment. When one claimed that his neighbor had encroached upon his boundaries, this new judge pacified him with the gift of a golden dish worth thrice the value of the disputed land, and he went away content.

For some time the novelty of her position and her freedom of sway afforded her all the amusement that she could ask; but after Ethelbald's first visit, she seemed restless.

"Is the realm of the West Saxons larger than this?" she asked of the king.

"Much larger," said he. "It is a fertile land, and it has wealth and wide boundaries, and its army can command twenty men to one of the land of Kent. It is a sad burden for a man to rule the kingdom of the West Saxons."

"Is the king's palace finer than this?" continued Judith.

"It is a great house," broke in Alfred, who had been eagerly listening, "and there were very many dishes of gold, and red and blue stones were around the edges; and the high seat in the hall was covered with purple and gold, and the pictures on the tapestries were of men and horses and water and boats; and the nixyman lives in the brook, and if you stop to look, he pulls you down; and the smith puts a rune on the sword when he likes his lord, and the flowers grow all around—" but the child stopped for want of breath.

"You remember well," said the king, smiling at his little son. "But do you not remember the church, too, Alfred, where the psalms were chanted every morning? But I have taught the singers here to chant as they do in Rome, Judith. The land of the West Saxons is a fair country, but the chanting is much better here. I am sure that you would like this land better."

Judith hardly heard his last words. She was gazing absently to the westward, and as if she had beckoned him to come, a rider appeared at the turn of the way. He came up slowly and was admitted into the palace. He bowed with deference to the king, then turned to the queen and said:—

"My lord the king of the West Saxons bade me bring you this." He glanced quickly at the king, and made his farewells as rapidly as possible. He had presented Judith with a little silken package bound with a slender gold chain. She held it silently for a moment and glanced at Ethelwulf. His face was calm and peaceful. She slipped off the gold chain and unfolded the silk. There lay a most exquisitely wrought mirror of polished silver set with clusters of amethysts. Under the mirror was a bit of parchment, and on it was written:—

"To the fairest of queens from one who admires her and would willingly—" That was all. Judith's face flushed scarlet, but King Ethelwulf was apparently much pleased.

"My son is a man of many interests," he said. "I suppose he could not stay with his scribe, and the lad forgot the rest of the message. He must have meant to write 'would willingly be his own messenger.' It is a pleasant courtesy, and we will send men to him with our thanks and a return gift before many days have passed."

But the first messenger that was sent to Ethelbald bore the sad tidings that the gentle old king was sick unto death. Judith, repenting the folly of her thought, was his most devoted attendant. The king was calm and happy. He had before this made his will, arranging for what he had no doubt was for the best good of his kingdom. Judith's kindness to Alfred assured him of the child's comfort, and he died peacefully without a shadow of unrest.

His will had been signed by some of the most powerful men among the West Saxons in token of their satisfaction with its provisions. He left Kent and the eastern district to Ethelbert, his second son, while Wessex, the most valuable part of the kingdom, was to remain in the hands of Ethelbald. If Ethelbald died leaving no children, Wessex was to come to Ethelred and then to Alfred. There was provision made for various deeds of charity for the benefit of his soul, and especially that one poor man in every ten of those living on his lands should be supplied with "meat, drink, and clothing," be he a native or foreigner—a rare bit of liberality in those times. This gift was to be continued by his successors "until the Day of Judgment, supposing, however, that the country should still be inhabited by men and cattle, and should not become deserted."

A long procession of truly sorrowing people followed the bier of Ethelwulf to his grave in Winchester cathedral. Then Judith and Alfred returned to the palace in Kent. Judith was sincerely grieved at the death of the kind-hearted old king, who had been to her a father rather than a husband, and she was even more kind than ever to her little stepson.

Ethelbert had taken his position as ruler of Kent. He was a gentle, quiet man, with all his father's sincerity, but he held quite different ideas of the duty of a king to his people. Ethelwulf had been contented if he heard no complaint; Ethelbert meant to see for himself that there was no ground for complaint. The result was that there were no more decisions made after the manner of Judith, for Ethelbert held the reins of his little kingdom gently but firmly, and he himself looked into all matters of dispute. The house of the noble and the straw-thatched cottage of the noble's workingman were both familiar to him, and in both was he equally welcome. His people felt for him the same love that they had felt for Ethelwulf, and they had a much greater confidence in his judgments, feeling that he knew his people as Ethelwulf had never known them.

Alfred was allowed to remain in Kent, much to Ethelbert's pleasure, but a little to his surprise.

Ethelbald had at first declared that the child should live with him, his lawful guardian; but suddenly he had checked himself, glanced at Judith, and yielded the point, saying:—

"As I am the boy's guardian, I shall pay him frequent visits."

Before many weeks, Judith's natural gayety and restlessness of disposition began to show itself. There seemed no place for her in the court of Ethelbert. He was kind and courteous, and apparently glad of her presence, but her taste of power had made her more restless than ever. She began to think that she would go back to her father's court, when her thoughts were suddenly turned back into an old channel from which they had seemed to have made their escape.

She was wandering about the skirts of the forest one day in early summer, Alfred her attendant as usual.

"I am tired," said Judith. "We'll sit down on this log, and I'll make you a crown of buttercups."

"Hilda made me a crown," said Alfred, "and then the robbers came, and they tied Hilda and hurt her; but they let me go, and didn't hurt me—"

"Oh!" exclaimed Judith, in a startled tone. Then quickly recovering herself, she said with her most dignified air:—

"Do you wish anything of the queen of Kent?"

An old woman bowed humbly before her. She wore a robe of dark brown or gray, so like the color of the trunks of the trees that she had wound her way among them without being seen until she was very near the queen and Alfred.

"The queen of Kent shall have a larger kingdom," she muttered in a low monotone, while her eyes were apparently gazing far away and she was making strange motions in the air with her fingers. The light and the dark did not strive; but the dark won, and the dark shall win."

There was something so uncanny in the woman's manner that for once Judith was really frightened. She arose and turned toward the palace, as if to summon aid. When she looked back again, the woman had gone as mysteriously as she had come.

Alfred had sat motionless during the interview, which indeed had lasted scarcely three minutes. He said:—

"I do not like that woman, Judith. I want to go home." They went toward the palace, both silent; but a spot of red burned on Judith's cheeks, as little by little the possible meaning of the old woman's speech came to her. From the secret place where she kept her treasures, she drew forth the bit of parchment and read:—

"One who admires her and would willingly—" Should she remain in Kent, or return to her own land—or should she defy the law of the church and the law of the land and become the queen of the West Saxons? She stood gazing at the bit of parchment when Alfred came to her.

"How does it say anything, Judith? Those queer marks haven't any sound. How does it talk? Won't you tell me how to hear it?"

"Yes, I will," said Judith. "I'll teach you to read and to write, and we'll begin now," for she was glad to have the matter out of her mind for even a little while.

From that time on for many days Alfred had his lesson in reading and writing every morning. There is a fine old English poem called "Judith," and it has been suggested that perhaps it was written in honor of this Judith's coming to England, and that maybe this was the book from which Alfred learned to read. It is the old story of Judith and Holofernes, captain of the Assyrians. Holofernes has subdued all the other people of the west country. He is now besieging the town of the Israelites and has gotten possession of their fountains of water. The Israelites agree to wait five days for help, and then, if the Lord does not aid them, they are determined to surrender. Judith sends for the leaders of the people and tells them that they must not limit God to five days, but must trust Him to save them. Something in her manner gives them confidence, and when she hints that she has thought of a way of salvation, they ask no questions, but go away begging her to pray for them.

Judith puts on her finest apparel and all her jewels and makes her way to the camp of the heathen. Holofernes is charmed with her beauty, and vows that he will carry her home to be the wife of his king; but at night, after a drunken revel, he falls into a stupor, and Judith and her maid draw aside the curtain of his tent, and Judith smites "twice upon his neck"; and the next morning, when as usual they leave the camp of the heathen to go out to pray, the maid carries in a basket the head of Holofernes.

Great is the rejoicing when the people on the walls of the beleaguered town see coming toward them "the maid of the Lord." They rush forth to meet her; and possibly these are the very lines whose complicated black letters and beautifully illuminated capitals Alfred's childish fingers may have traced in his efforts to "hear what the marks say."

> The army rejoiced,
> The people pressed to the fortress gate,
> Women and men together; in crowds,
> In multitudes, masses, they surged and they thronged,
> Old men and young men running by thousands,
> To meet the maid of the Lord; and the heart
> Of every man in the city rejoiced
> That Judith had come again to her homeland.
> Straightway they flung wide the gates and gave welcome,
> With reverence they bade her to enter the city.

Ethelbert was not quite sure that it was wise for his little brother to learn to read and write, for his father had known how to read, and had he not lost his kingdom? but the child pleaded so earnestly, and Judith's argument that a king ought to be able to sign his name to state documents was so convincing, that he yielded, and Alfred went on happily, to Judith's pleasure as well as his.

But the question that was weighing so heavily upon Judith returned again and again, and at last one who knew of it might have guessed from the touch of recklessness in her manner that it had been decided, even before Ethelbald came to her for his brief and determined wooing.

A stronger man than Ethelbald would have followed the right way; a weaker man would have had many misgivings. Ethelbald was not strong enough to do right, and he was not weak enough to hesitate. In this, as in everything else, he carried matters with a high hand. Before he came to Judith, he had had a stormy interview with one of his bishops. As he had raised the prelate to his present position, the king had no doubt of his ability to control his priest. With coat of mail and sword he strode into the chamber of the bishop.

"I propose to wed Judith, queen of Kent," he said bluntly.

"Such a marriage is against the custom of the land and the law of the church," said the bishop firmly.

"Then I'll marry her without the custom of the land and the law of the church," said Ethelbald.

"It was for breaking the law that your father lost his kingdom," said the bishop.

"My father lost his kingdom because he was not strong enough to hold it," said Ethelbald.

"Think you," asked the bishop quietly, "that the king of the Franks would permit his daughter to wed without the blessing of the church?"

"The king of the Franks has all that he can do to remain king of the Franks," sneered Ethelbald. "He will not interfere with the land of the West Saxons. But you talk of breaking the laws of the church. Was it not breaking her laws for a man to draw back after he had begun to be a priest?"

"Your father had the dispensation of the Pope because of the unforeseen needs of the kingdom," said the bishop.

"Very well," said Ethelbald, "get as many dispensations as you like, and pay the price; endow a church if you choose. One never knows what whim a woman may take into her head, and if the fair Judith fancies a dispensation instead of a jewel, it is the same to me; only it will be a day late, for if the queen of Kent agrees, she shall be queen of the West Saxons within a month, and you shall say the words that make her my wife."

"Never," said the bishop firmly.

The king drew his sword. "Do you know that if I take your life this moment, there is not one man in my kingdom who will dare call me to account?"

"The life of the priest is at the service of the church," said the bishop, glancing indifferently at the drawn sword.

"So that's it, is it?" said Ethelbald. "Then the priest may have his life, but he shall not have his church. Promise me here upon the cross that when I bring to you her who is to be queen of the West Saxons, you will say over us the words that make her my wife and that you will pronounce upon us the blessing of the church. Refuse, and I swear to you here by my sword that before the next coming of the new moon there shall not be a church standing in the land of the West Saxons. Choose." The bishop paled.

"I know whereof I speak," said Ethelbald. "There are men in my pay who would burn a church as willingly as a heap of brushwood." The bishop knew that this was true.

"Choose," thundered Ethelbald. The bishop sank trembling upon a bench.

"I yield," he said. "I will say the words that make you man and wife. The sin be mine; the churches are saved. Other men have given their lives for the church; I have given my soul."

"You will pronounce the blessing of the church?" persisted Ethelbald mercilessly.

"I will," said the bishop, as a deathly pallor spread over his face.

"Here's your pay," said the king, tossing him a bag of gold coins, a rarity in the Saxon kingdom. It fell upon the floor. The bishop roused himself and gave the little bag a most unbishoply kick out of the open door.

"Thy gold perish with thee," he whispered sharply, as he sank back again on the bench. Ethelbald laughed.

"I like your pluck," said he. "It's a pity that you had to give in, but I really don't see that you had any way out of it."

As soon as the proposed marriage was known over the kingdom, there was a stern wrath and indignation manifested that would have warned a man far less keen than the king that the utmost which even he dared attempt was a quiet ceremony with none of the customary feasting and rejoicing.

Alfred was broken-hearted at losing Judith, and at last Ethelbert sent for Swithin to try to comfort him. The bishop told him as clearly as he could tell a child of nine years that Judith had done what was wrong.

"You do not wish to live with a woman who would teach you to do wrong, do you, Alfred?" the bishop questioned gently.

"No," said Alfred, "but I want my Judith. I do want my Judith."

Chapter VIII.

Who Shall Be King?

Ethelbald had intended that Alfred should live with him, but here Bishop Swithin interposed and to some purpose.

"King Ethelbald," he said, "you well know the feeling of your people. It is no stronger in Wessex than it is in Kent. The people of Kent love the child and are proud of having him among them. Take him away and they will—"

"Revolt?" said the king contemptuously. "Against whom? My brother Ethelbert has done nothing to arouse their anger. Let them attack me if they choose; I can crush any outbreak that the little realm of Kent can make."

"True," said the bishop, "you can, if you think it wise to try to subdue a domain that is not yours. You can lay the land of your brother waste, if you will; but in so doing you destroy the eastern bulwark against the Danes and open the way for them to march without let or hindrance into the heart of the country."

Ethelbald was quick to see where he must yield. "Have your own way then," he said. "Alfred is a child now, but when he is twelve, he comes to me. Understand that, will you? and if you have not made him into a psalm-singing churchman like yourselves, I will teach him how to be a prince and a soldier."

"There is a psalm-singing churchman called Alstan who once showed himself the best soldier in England," said the bishop quietly. "And there was once a psalm-singing Pope who fortified Rome and saved her from the attacks of the heathen."

"You priests always have the last word," sneered Ethelbald, "but the boy comes to me at twelve; there's no power in England to prevent that."

"There is a Power above England," said the bishop reverently, as Ethelbald strode away.

It was fortunate, perhaps, that Alfred was not asked with which one of his brothers he preferred to live, for it would have been very hard for him to choose. Ethelbald, who had fought in a real battle had always been looked upon with wonder and admiration by the little boy, who was so much younger than he; and Judith, the lovable, fascinating Judith, was with him in Wessex. Nothing would make up for the loss of Judith. But Alfred believed every word that Bishop Swithin said, and the bishop told him that Judith had done wrong, and that she would teach him to be a wicked man. Then, too, he had become very fond of Ethelbert, who seemed to him rather like a father than a brother, for Ethelbert's own children were not so many years younger than Alfred himself. Alfred loved these children and was happy with them, and in spite of his longing for Judith, he became before many days had passed the same cheerful little boy that he had always been.

Their life in Kent went on peacefully and quietly until the year 860 came and Alfred was nearly twelve years of age. Although Alfred knew nothing about it, Ethelbald had never given up his intention to have the boy come to him, and in every communication from the king of the West Saxons there was some mention made of the plan. Ethelbald had no child, and he had taken a dislike to Ethelred. The mild, wavering, undecided disposition of the younger brother had always annoyed Ethelbald, and he was determined that he would prevent Ethelred from succeeding to the throne of the West Saxons, and would train Alfred to be a prince after his own heart and to govern the kingdom as he himself governed it.

Bishop Swithin was greatly troubled about the matter. It was bad enough to have his little favorite put into the hands of a usurper, but to have the child himself taught to usurp the throne of the West Saxons when it belonged of right to his older brother would bring on revolt and disaster. The Danes would pounce down upon a country divided and at strife. Fire and rapine and murder, a devastated land, a king fleeing for his life or else become a victim of the Danish onslaught, churches torn down, convents burned, the land become a wilderness through which the wild beasts roamed fearlessly—when the bishop pictured all this to himself, it is no wonder that his heart sank. It was night. Hour after hour he lay awake. At last he rose, went into the chapel, and flung himself down before the altar.

"O God," he prayed, "the child is Thine, save him from those that would lead him astray. The land is Thine, save it for Thyself and Thy truth. Let not the child bring darkness and wrong upon his country; let him bring light and—" There was a thundering knock at the door, but the bishop in his anguish of soul did not heed it.

"The bishop! We must see the bishop," a loud voice cried.

"The bishop is at prayer," said the keeper of the door. "I shall not disturb him unless you come from the king."

"Tell him," cried the messenger, "that we come from the dead body of him that was king of the West Saxons." The bishop had heard the last words.

"God be thanked," said he, and then stopped in horror. "A wicked man has died in his sins. God pardon him," he said. "There is, indeed, a Power that rules over England," and he went forth to meet the messenger.

Ethelbald had fallen from his horse and had died almost instantly, and the counselors were in a difficulty. By Ethelwulf's will Ethelbert was to remain king of Kent, Surrey, and Sussex; and Ethelred was to follow Ethelbald as king of the West Saxons. Now in Ethelbald's plans that Alfred should succeed him, Ethelred had never been allowed to take his proper position as crown prince. To the people at large he was almost unknown. Alstan was far away on a journey. What to do for the best good of the land lay in the hands of the bishop and the company of counselors that followed hard upon the messenger. There at midnight in the bishop's chapel the fate of the kingdom was discussed.

"By the king's will to which we agreed," said one, "Ethelred should be king of the West Saxons."

"True," said another, "but matters are changed. When Ethelwulf died, the land was at peace. A child could have ruled the country. It is different now. There are rumors of the restlessness of the Danes. Should they come down upon our shores again, no gentle hand can defend us. We need a strong arm and a wise head. Bishop Swithin, you know the princes. Is Ethelred strong and wise and brave and fearless? Will he dare to give us justice in peace? Will he lead us worthily against our foes?"

"Ethelred—" began the bishop slowly, but the sound of hurrying horsemen was heard. A man who had been on guard rushed in breathlessly.

"I heard their words," he gasped. "They go to tell the princes of the death of the king."

"What we do must be done quickly," said one, with an impatient glance at the bishop, who stood silent, his eyes bent on the ground. At last the bishop spoke.

"The king must be one of the three," he said. "Alfred is too young, Ethelred is not the strong hand that should rule the land. I know, perhaps even more than you, of her dangers. We break the letter of Ethelwulf's will to favor no usurper, but to keep its spirit rather than its letter. I counsel that Ethelbert be made king of the West Saxons."

In a moment the counselors were on their horses and pressing onward to overtake those who were in advance of them. The sun was fully overhead when they reached the palace of King Ethelbert. The two parties of riders had chanced to take different roads in the forest and approached the palace from nearly opposite directions.

"We would see King Ethelbert," cried the counselors that had gone to the bishop.

"We demand to see Ethelred, *our king,*" shouted the others.

In the presence of the three brothers there was a stormy scene. One party demanded the literal execution of the king's will; the other pleaded the needs of the kingdom. Ethelbert was thoughtful; Ethelred irresolute, at one moment ready to seize the throne that had been willed to him, and the next drawing back from the dangers and difficulties that lay before him who should rule the West Saxons. Many looked upon Alfred, the prince who had made the pilgrimage to Rome and who had been blessed by the Pope, and wished that he was older; but Alfred thought only of the death of his brother, his warrior brother, who had been his ideal of all that was strong and bold and warlike.

"They all go away from me," he said to himself, "my mother, my father, my sister, Judith, and now my brother—" but Ethelbert was speaking.

"There has never been discord among the sons of Ethelwulf," he said. "My brothers and myself will withdraw to an inner chamber and consult. Do you agree to await our decision and to abide by it?" One party said "Yes" frankly and willingly, the other slowly and doubtfully, but all felt that nothing better could be done. When the brothers were alone, Ethelbert said:—

"Ethelred, the kingdom of the West Saxons is yours by our father's will. Do you take it? Will you rule the people in peace and lead them in war?"

"Yes," said Ethelred, "I will take it."

"You know," said Ethelbert, "that it is a divided kingdom. Some would have you for king, some would have me, and some look with affection upon our younger brother and wish that it might fall into his hands before many years have passed. Can you meet this opposition?" Ethelred hesitated.

"This is not a new question to me," said Ethelbert. "Many weeks ago, two trusty counselors came to me and said that Ethelbald was in danger of his life as much from his own recklessness as from secret enemies. They told me that it would be the wish of many that I, who had had some experience in ruling, should take the throne of the West Saxons as well as that of Kent and the eastern districts, and hold it as a trust, not for my children, but for you, and after you, Alfred: that so the two kingdoms might gain in strength by union and that you who are younger might have years and experience before meeting your time of danger and responsibility. Do you agree to that, Ethelred?"

"I agree," said Ethelred, always ready to agree to the last speech.

"Alfred, do you agree that I shall take the throne of the West Saxons and that you shall not rule until after I and Ethelred are dead?"

"My father told me never to wish to be king before my brothers," said Alfred simply.

And so a parchment was written saying that Ethelred and Alfred waived their right to the rule of the West Saxons during the life of their older brother. When the parchment was passed to Alfred and he was told to make his mark, he said:—

"But I can write my name," and as the gray old counselors pressed near to see the wonderful thing, the boy slowly and laboriously wrote his name, "as well as a clerk could have done it," the counselors said.

There was great sorrow in the land of Kent when it was known that Ethelbert, though still their king, was to dwell chiefly in the region of the West Saxons, for his mild and just rule had made him very dear to them in the two years that he had held the kingdom. They were still more sorry because Alfred must go with him, for they had become very fond of the child; but there was no help for it, and Ethelbert and his two brothers removed to Alfred's old home at Wantage in Berkshire.

They had the long, pleasant sail on the river that Alfred remembered so well at the beginning of his great journey to Rome. He knew the very place where his father had spurred on his horse and dashed away into the woods; but perhaps the most vivid picture in his mind was of his mother as she stood in the door of the palace and bade him her last farewell; and as they rode up to the house, he felt for the jewel which hung on a light golden chain around his neck. As he touched it, he could almost believe that Osburga was with him, and was glad to have him return to the house that was so closely associated with her memory.

Little was changed about the place. Alfred wandered about, over the bridge where he used to fear the nixyman, to see the horses and dogs, to the bakery and to the smithy. Everywhere was a warm greeting for him.

"And have you lost the sword that I made you?" asked the smith.

"No, surely," said Alfred, "but it is too small now. Will you make me a larger one? And I want a spear too, for Ethelbert says I may go on a real boar-hunt when I am fourteen."

"And will you have a rune on your sword?" asked the smith with a sly twinkle in his eye.

"Bishop Swithin says that prayers are better than runes," said Alfred, "and he gave me this and told me to carry it with me always," and he drew forth from the bosom of his tunic a tiny parchment book of psalms and prayers.

"And can you really tell what the marks say?" asked the old blacksmith, gazing eagerly at the marvel.

"Judith taught me to read English," said Alfred, "and I can read the Latin a very little, but I know all this by heart. But when will you make me the spear? Will you do it right away? See how tall I am. I shall be fourteen before very long."

"Yes," said the smith. "And I'll put a rune on it too," he muttered as the child went away, "though I'm afraid that all this praying will spoil it."

Ethelbert had no time to think of boar-hunts, for there was much to be done in his new kingdom. First, he gave to the cathedral at Sherborne, where Ethelbald was buried, forty pounds of silver, three golden crosses, and land enough to feed one thousand swine. This gift for the repose of his brother's soul was from his own private property; and he also promised to give every year one hundred marks that prayers might be offered for Ethelbald and psalms sung once a week through the year.

The churches had suffered throughout Wessex, for Ethelbald had no interest in them, and he had taken as large a portion of their revenues as he dared to apply to other purposes. Ethelbert felt that his next business must be to right the wrongs that had been done them.

The defenses of the realm were in good order, for Ethelbald had strengthened them continually. In some respects his fighting men had been well prepared for fighting. They had weapons of one kind or another, and they knew how to use them. Even those who most disliked Ethelbald were proud of him, for he had taught them how to fight and how to follow a leader, and they were ready to plunge into any kind of danger, if there was but one brave man to go before them.

Even in the first few months of Ethelbert's reign, danger was nearer than any one thought, for a fleet of Danish boats had silently made their way down the English Channel. The Danes had meant to land boldly on Thanet, but a dense fog came up that suggested their passing by the eastern coast in the darkness, and then landing either on the Frankish shores or in southern England, as the wind might blow them. Storm or sunshine, it was all the same to them. They did not care for conquest and settlement, but only to burn and kill and go away laden with booty. They boasted that they slept under no roof and sat by no hearth. One son must stay at home to inherit and care for the ancestral property, but the others took the sea for their kingdom. The ship and the sword were their riches, and bracelets set with many jewels, which stood to them for bravery rather than for beauty, for they were the spoils of fighting, and on them their most solemn oaths were sworn. Their unwritten law was that a Dane must attack two and stand firm against three. He might retire one pace from four, but he must not fly for fewer than five. They knew no fear, and sought eagerly for a violent death, for he who would enter the halls of Odin must have died in battle, and his rank among the dead heroes depended upon the number of men that he had slain.

These were the people that under cover of the fog glided along the southern coast of England as far as the Isle of Wight. At the mouth of the Itchen River a pause was made.

"I have heard," said Weland, their leader, "that not many miles up this stream is a town with churches and convents and treasures of gold and silver and jewels and—" Shouts of delight from his followers interrupted him. "There are black-robed monks who pray against us to their gods till even Thor himself could not give us the victory. There are books with magical marks, and even our greatest runes have no power against them. Burn the books, kill the monks, and win your place in the halls of Odin. The coward falls to the realm of death and to the ninth world below death, to the darkness of the forgotten; but when the brave man dies, the Valkyrs go forth to meet him, and bear him with song and the clangor of sword and shield to Valhalla, and there he feasts with the gods forever and forever. Will ye be cowards or heroes? Will ye feast with the gods, or will ye go to the land of the forgotten and be as if ye never were? Let every man lay his hand upon the bracelets that he won by his valor and swear to be braver than ever before, or let him never dream of the joys of Valhalla, for with my own hand I will fling him off yonder cliff that he may die the death of the coward that he is."

Wild shouts of eagerness for the attack and defiance of their enemies rang through the foggy air.

"Then hear my words," said Weland. "Keep close to the shore under the shadow of the trees until we are in sight of the town. Then let not a word be spoken. Let not a sound be heard. Let no dry twig break under foot. Let no bird be disturbed in her nest as we go through the woods. When we come to the town, take your stand as I shall bid you; and then let no man stir from his place until Balder smiles upon our quest for glory. When I give the signal at the first ray of the sun, shout defiance, sing the song

IN THE EARLY GRAY OF THE MORNING THEY COULD SEE ... THE OUTLINES OF THE HIGHEST BUILDINGS.

of Odin, the lord of battles, and follow the leader. Burn, kill, seize treasures, win your seats in the halls of the mighty."

The fog lifted, but protected by the night, the pirates rowed silently up the stream in their light boats. In the early gray of the morning, they could see vaguely against the eastern sky the outlines of the highest buildings. Forests were here and there in gloomy masses wherein no ray of light had penetrated. Beyond them were low-lying hills. There were rich pasture lands and cultivated fields, and in the midst of it was the quiet little town through which the river peacefully flowed.

Not a sound was heard; the village was sleeping fearlessly. Silently as a pestilence the Danes made their way up from the grassy shores of the river. Under the whispered commands of their leader, they divided into two parties. One party went softly around the town to the extreme west; the other took their stand on the little bridge that Bishop Swithin had built, little thinking that it would ever serve as a vantage ground for their foes.

There was a moment of stillness. Even a fiend might have pitied the little village sleeping so trustfully in the first gray glimmerings of the morning. Light mists showed the course of the river winding gently through the meadows. The willows bending over it took on a tinge of green. A gentle breeze brought the freshness of the forest to the men standing like statues on the bridge and at the western side of the town. A bird chirped sleepily. The church towers grew more distinct every moment. Far away on the hills a cock crowed, and from a still more distant hill an answer came. A dog barked, but his master only grumbled sleepily at being disturbed. The light grew stronger; the east was all aglow. The first ray of the sun shot over the hills.

"The gods be with us!" cried the Danes, and with shrieks of fiendish ecstasy they fell upon the defenseless village.

Chapter IX.

After the Massacre

It was bright and sunny. The sky was blue and cloudless, and the birds were flitting about merrily from tree to tree. After the many days of fog and dampness, the green of the leaves and the grass shone out fresher and clearer than ever. The cattle were lying in the shade of the trees, and the sheep were nibbling busily in the upland pastures. The river flowed on with cheery little murmurs of content as it rippled over the stones under Swithin's bridge. Here and there a slender stream of red dropped sullenly into the sparkling waters, but the river flowed on, caring as little for the drops of blood as if they had been but the reflection of some of the crimson flowers that bent over the tranquil pools where the sunny water slipped into some curve of the shore under the willows for a little visit before making its great journey to the sea.

In the midst of the beauty and the brightness lay the remains of what had been the town of Winchester. Desolation and ruin were everywhere. Houses were torn down and burned. Wherever one looked was fire or smouldering brands. The dead lay where they fell, some in their own doorways where they had died in helpless defense of their homes, some even in their beds where the Danes had cut them down with no chance for even one blow in return. Some lay in the streets where they had fallen fighting bravely and hopelessly for their town and their people. Here lay the body of a woman who had been killed by a Danish sword as she tried to save her child. The baby lay dead not far from its mother, gashed in many places where the Danes had tossed it on their spears in their fiendish sport.

Happy were those that had fallen, for the living, maimed and wounded, were moaning piteously in their sorrow and agony. Horses, tortured in wanton brutality and left to die, roamed wildly up and down the streets, and sometimes one would hear that rare, almost human cry of the suffering creature. Here and there a dog, perhaps bleeding and whining with pain, but always faithful, was slowly dragging himself about, sniffing at one dead body and then at another, lifting up his head with a long howl of disappointment and grief, as he failed to find the master whom he was seeking.

This was the work of the Danes in the few hours of their onslaught upon the defenseless town. The cathedral stood apparently uninjured, though in front of its door had been some of the hardest fighting, for the Saxons had not yielded without a struggle, hopeless as it was from the very beginning.

The Danes had forced their way into the church, singing wild songs of Odin and Thor. The heavy doors had made a few minutes' delay, which the priests had seized to try to hide away some of their treasures.

"Bring out your gold! Bring out your jewels!" cried the Danes. The priests were silent. Weapons of defense there were none. They could only suffer and die.

"Bring out your books of magic!" cried Weland. Not a priest moved.

"Let us take them home for slaves," said one.

"Never," said another, "they will pray to their gods against us. See!" for the priests were murmuring fervent prayers, their eyes turned up to heaven.

"You think you see your god coming? You shall not see him if he comes," cried the first, as with a stroke of his sword he blinded the one that was nearest. There was a mad shriek of delight from a distant corner. The robbers had found the golden vessels and the jewels, and the vestments embroidered with silk and adorned with precious stones. One of the Danes sprang upon the altar and seized the golden pyx wherein lay the consecrated wafer. In an instant, the priest that was nearest felled him with his naked fist. Still clutching the pyx, he rolled down the steps to the floor of the chancel. The holy bread fell from its place. The priest, with a hasty prayer, put it reverently between his lips. All this was done in a moment. It was the signal for a general massacre, and in a few minutes every priest lay dead on the floor of his cathedral.

The Danes roamed at will through the building, piling up the treasures in a great heap; then loading themselves with gold and silver vessels, golden chains, jeweled vases, and embroidered robes, they made their way out, singing songs of defiance of all men save their leader and of all gods save their own.

There was no one to resist them as they sped toward the place a little way down the river where they had left their boats concealed under the overhanging branches. The woods rang with wild songs of the glory of their exploits. Loaded down as they were, they soon had to delay their steps and wend their way more slowly through the forest, but they were safe from all attack; why should they hasten? They would be on their vessels that were waiting at the mouth of the river long before any word could go to the king and a force be sent to oppose them. So they went their way with minds at ease to the place where they had left their boats. With a howl of rage and amazement, they saw that the boats were gone.

Now, while the Danes were coming up the river, it happened

that a young lad who lived not far from Winchester was passing a very restless night. The one thing for which he cared was hunting, and he was happy whether he was pursuing deer or wolves or foxes, or even such small game as hares. There was no one else in Winchester that knew the woods as well as he. Every little by-path was as familiar to him as his own town. For many miles around, there was hardly a spot where he could not have been set down by night or day and have found his way home with perfect ease. Now this lad had invented a rabbit-trap that he was sure would be better than those of his companions; and as the night passed on, he grew more and more impatient to see what its success had been on this, its first trial.

When daybreak was not more than an hour or two distant, this lad slipped out of the house and made his way through the dark and gloomy woods to his traps. He found them readily and was just about to whistle his delight at finding them full, when he fancied that he saw heavy, moving shadows between him and the less dense darkness of the river. He stood motionless. His ear, trained by his outdoor life to catch the least sound, heard even the light tread of the invaders on the dry twigs. He heard a whispered command. Softly he swung himself up into a tree and clung to it, hardly daring to breathe, until the long line of men had gone far beyond his sight and hearing. His life in the woods had made him quickwitted. The Danes had taken the shortest route to the town, and there was no way to give warning. All that he could do was to find the ealderman of the district and trust that men could come in time, if not to save the little town, at least to avenge it.

As he slipped noiselessly from his perch in the tree, the thought occurred to him that there was one other thing that he could do. He made his way to the river, it might have been at the peril of his life, for he did not know that the Danes had not left a guard; but no sound was heard, and no one rose up out of the gray darkness to confront him. The night was a shade lighter, and he could see the dim mass of a boat, another, and another. Still fearful that any sound might betray him, he dropped silently into the stream, his hunting-knife between his teeth, and swam to one boat and another, cutting each one adrift. Then he shook himself dry like a great water-dog, and started for Osric, ealderman of Hants.

The boy's knowledge of the country served him well. Where others would have walked, he ran; where others would have slowly picked their way down the steep hillside, he leaped from rock to rock. He had no fear of anything in the world, saving only the Danes. The thought of them spurred him on, and in half the time that any one else would have needed, he was at the manor of Osric, the chief man of Hants, so exhausted that he could hardly gasp out:—

"The Danes—Winchester!"

Such a message as that needed little explanation. A horseman was on his way to Ethelwulf, ealderman of Berkshire, and another to King Ethelbert, even before the boy could tell any more of his story.

Fate favored the avengers, for as Osric's men drew near the mouth of the river, only half of the robber band were near them, floating leisurely down the stream, while the others were working their way painfully through the forest.

When the Danes examined the river banks more closely, they found that part of their boats had been caught in the reeds and the low branches that overhung the water. These were easily recovered by their owners. Those who came to them first crowded in with their treasures till the boats sank to the water's edge. It was evident that some of the party would float comfortably to their vessels; others must work their way through the tangled wilderness, bearing the loads that taxed even their strength, accustomed as they were to brief fights, but not to long-enduring labors. A quarrel arose. Some of the murderers were killed in the strife. Those that were stronger seized the boats and floated away, leaving the others to come to the mouth of the river as best they could.

All this time Osric and his men were coming down upon them as fast as horses could carry them, and not far behind the soldiers of Hants were the men of Ethelwulf, and a little farther back was King Ethelbert himself with many men.

Alfred had begged earnestly to go with the fighting men.

"I could help, Ethelbert," he pleaded, "I am sure I could. You know I shot that raven on the wing yesterday."

"To fight Danes one needs other weapons than bows and arrows," said Ethelbert kindly, as he hurriedly fastened on his armor, "and fighting robbers and murderers is not for boys, but for strong men."

"But it was a boy who brought the news. He did something for his people," said Alfred, but Ethelred shook his head and rode away with his men.

Alfred went disconsolately out to his friend the blacksmith.

"You needn't make me any sword," said he. "I'm only a boy, and they think I'm nothing; but you know I am strong. I always throw the others at the wrestling, and I can run faster and leap further than any one else. I know I could have helped."

The smith looked silently at the well-knit but slender frame of the boy. Then he took from the further corner of his smithy a heavy battle-axe.

"This is what the Danes fight with," said he. "Can you lift

it?" Alfred tried in vain. "Could you wrestle with men who can use that? or could you strike with a sword ten times as heavy as yours? Learn how to use weapons now, and by and by strength will come."

"I'm sure I could have done something, though," said Alfred, and he wandered about in a very gloomy mood. Bishop Swithin discovered him where he had thrown himself on the grass under a tree, and in a moment guessed what was the trouble.

"It is hard for both of us," he said quietly. "Why, can't you go if you want to?" asked the boy looking up quickly.

"No. It is possible that our men may not get the better of the Danes, and that they may press on even into the heart of Wessex. I have promised King Ethelbert to stay here with his helpless children to aid and advise if need comes."

"But you can do something," said Alfred, "and I can do nothing. I cannot even go to try."

"And do you think that I do not want to go to my poor people in Winchester?" said the bishop. "Oh, if I could only have been with them to try to defend them and to die with them if I failed!"

Alfred was not really comforted, however, until the triumphant return of the king, when he learned that all the fighting had been over before they could reach the scene of action.

"Never before had a king such brave thegns," exclaimed Ethelbert in an outburst of generous admiration. "Osric knew only too well that it was too late to do any good in Winchester, and he set off at full speed for the mouth of the river. It was rashness itself, for he expected to meet the whole company of the robbers. As it was, the Danes separated, no one knows why, not far below Winchester. Their boats were loaded down with treasure from the cathedral"—here Swithin groaned involuntarily—"and even their skill could hardly keep them afloat. Osric's men gave them a storm of spears, the boats capsized, and almost in a moment many a death in the town had been avenged."

"Did any of them get away?" asked Alfred.

"What few were left alive ran for their ships. They waded and swam, throwing off their swords and battle-axes in their flight, and reached their boats; but hidden in them were the rest of Osric's men, and as the Danes climbed up over the side, a blow from a sword or an axe put an end to them, and every one of those that came by boat was killed."

"And those that came by land," said Swithin; "what became of them?"

"They seem to have come slowly through the forest," said the king, "but no one knows why, for it is not the custom of the Danes to come in vessels too large to go up any stream, nor is it their wont to divide a company in this way. God favored us, that is all I can say," said the king reverently. "The other party came out from the forest into the open just as Ethelwulf's men came in sight. Our men on the ships could see that the Danes far outnumbered the Saxons, so they sprang overboard and hastened ashore to help in the fight. This was even more bloody than the other, for the Danes had seen some signs of battle, and were not so unprepared as were the first party. They fought bravely at first, but in the midst of the fighting a strange thing happened. The wind had blown a roll of manuscript to the feet of their leader. He stepped on it, slipped, and fell. In a moment he recovered himself, but Osric says that he never saw such a look of fear and horror on any one's face. What could it mean?"

"The Danes fear that evil spirits live in books," said Swithin.

"They fled like sheep," said Ethelbert, "and when our party came in sight, those that were alive had scrambled into their vessels and were gone."

"And now I must go to my suffering people," said Swithin, rising eagerly.

"Swift horses and an escort shall be ready for you at any moment," said the king; and added as he pressed the hand of the old man:—

"The one happy thing about this terrible time is that you were here with us and are safe."

"Thank you, my king," said the bishop brokenly; "but my people, O my people!"

Months went on and the Danes made no other attempt to invade the land of the West Saxons. Ethelbert was occupied with manifold cares, but he did not forget his little brother, for he, as well as Ethelbald, had ideas of how a prince should be trained. Boys in noble families were taught as a matter of course to serve their elders, to be courteous and obedient. He must learn to play on the harp, for a noble who could not play was looked upon as a boor. Alfred begged to be taught to read Latin more perfectly, but this seemed utterly useless to Ethelbert, and, too, there was no one to teach him. Books were written in Latin, but there was almost no one to read what few were in the kingdom. The service of the church was in Latin, but though the priests pronounced the words, few had a very definite idea of their meaning. So Alfred learned little of books, but he did learn hunting and hawking, how to catch birds in snares, how to lie flat in the bottom of his boat hidden under branches of trees till he was near enough to the wild birds to shoot them with his bow and arrow. He learned to wrestle and run and leap, and how to use spear and shield and sword and battle-axe; and a few months before he was fourteen, Ethelbert allowed him to go on his first boar-hunt.

The hunters met in the great open space in front of the palace door. They were on horseback, and most of them wore green

THE FURIOUS BEAST DASHED AT THE
HORSE THAT BORE THE PRINCE.

tunics and many had small caps. They all carried spears. The dogs were leaping around them, and Alfred was as delighted as they, for ever since the days when his father's thegn had dashed through the forest with him on the front of his saddle and had killed a wild pig, he had longed to go on a hunt.

At last the signal was given. Into the woods they rushed. The huntsmen blew their horns, the dogs bayed, and the horses sprang forward.

"They have found him," was the shout, as a deep peculiar tone came from the dogs, and on the riders rushed more wildly than ever.

"My prince, my prince," shouted Beortric, who had been intrusted with the care of Alfred, for the excited boy was far ahead of the others.

"The prince will be killed," he cried, and urged on his horse. Far ahead of them was a little open space, and there they could see the young prince, his little cap fallen from his head, and his long yellow hair tossing in the sunshine, as he charged upon the boar again and again. The furious beast dashed at the horse that bore the prince. The horse sprang to one side, the boy's spear fell from his hand, and he himself rose in his stirrups, then seemed to totter. Beortric and the others were pressing wildly on. Beortric shut his eyes that he might not see the death of his prince, and rode on madly. But there were wild shouts of applause. The fearless boy had swung himself lightly from his horse's back into the branches of a great oak, and was crying:—

"A spear! Give me a spear!" The dogs were down below him. The boar was at bay, but was growing weaker at every course. The hunters sprang forward with their spears leveled.

"Hold!" shouted Beortric, "it is the prince's quarry. Give him a spear, he shall kill the boar," and in a few minutes the boy was standing flushed and happy, with his spear in his hand, and the great dead boar lying beside him.

There was much rejoicing when the tired, dusty company road home, dragging the boar. King Ethelbert gave a great feast in honor of the prince's first exploit. There were chickens and fish and eels, and hot cakes made of wheaten flour, and wine and ale and morat and pigment. There was venison and pork and beef and hares and mutton, but the great dish was the roasted flesh of the boar that Alfred had killed. When this was brought in and put at the head of the table, the harpers sang a song, praising the deed of the little prince. Ethelbert put a knife into the boy's hand and showed him how to make the first cut. For hours the feasting went on, but in the midst of it a message came from Winchester:—

"Swithin, the bishop, is sick unto death, and would fain see the sons of Ethelwulf before he dies." In a moment the reveling ceased; horses were brought, and in the early gray of the morning the king and his brothers set forth to say farewell to the good bishop who had been the true friend of their father and of his father before him. Long before they came to Winchester, a second messenger came crying:—

"Hasten, if you would see him alive." They hurried on at full speed, but it was almost too late. The bishop recognized the sons of his old friend, but he could not speak. He clasped feebly the hand of each of the three brothers in his own, and died holding Alfred's hand and with his eyes full of affection fixed upon the boy's face.

It was a sad journey back to Wantage. The bishop had been buried as in his humbleness of spirit he had requested, not in the church, but outside it, between the church and the belfry tower, where the drippings from the eaves might fall upon it, and where it might be trodden on by passers-by. Here in the cathedral lay his old friend, King Egbert, and Egbert's son, Ethelwulf, who had been scarcely less dear to him. There was the little stone bridge that he had built, repaired after the ravages of the Danes, and already the people were telling stories of the miracles that had been wrought upon it, that a poor woman had slipped and broken a basketful of eggs, and the bishop had restored them at a touch. Then they recalled his custom of going barefooted when he was called upon to dedicate a church, and of going in the night lest the people should gather around him to do him honor, as was their wont.

Slowly and sadly the brothers went on their homeward way. Their long train followed, and there was not one among them that did not mourn sincerely for the dead bishop.

Chapter X.

On the Island of Thanet

On the northeast coast of Thanet, at the very edge of the chalk-cliffs, two men were pacing up and down. They bore light arms, but evidently their dress was arranged for speed rather than for fighting, for their tunics were short, their cloaks were warm but light, and they wore no coats of mail. Apparently they were on guard, for they kept close watch of the sea from the long lines of breakers that rolled up at the base of the cliff to the far northern horizon.

"What do you think of that cloud far to the northeast?" asked the older.

"As you yourself say, that it is a cloud," responded the other lightly, "or it may be a great school of fish that ripple the surface and darken it. It is the time of year for sudden flaws and changes of the wind, and by the chill in the air it may be one of the northern snowstorms that has lost its way and is coming down upon us."

"It is too far away for either fish or a gust of wind to darken the water," replied the other. "Perhaps I am too fearful of danger, but it is a lesson that I have learned through hard experience."

"I know," said the younger man, with quick sympathy, "that you have suffered sorely from them. What a land we might have if we were free from fear of the heathen! It was at a time of feasting, was it not, that they came down upon you?"

"Yes," said the older. "It was in the autumn, Our corn had been harvested, our fruits and vegetables stored for the winter. Even the children were happy in the nuts that they had gathered, and the berries that they had dried for the colder months. We had asked our kinsfolk to come to us for a feast. We sat at the table, we ate and we drank and we were happy. The brother of my father was a thegn of King Ethelwulf, a brave man whom the king delighted to honor, and out of respect to him the king had sent his own harper to the feast. He was singing to us the old song of Beowulf and the fire-breathing dragon that our forefathers used to sing centuries ago in the days when they lived across the water, when there were dragons and caves of treasures and dens of monsters under the sea. In those times a man might go forth and fight his foes, and know that his wife and children were safe at home; but now it is the wife and children who are tortured and slain, while the man lies helpless."

"Every one sympathizes with the sufferings of Eardwulf, and there is not a man in the land of the Saxons who does not honor you for your bravery," said the younger man earnestly.

"I killed six. Would that it had been sixty," said Eardwulf "but then my sword failed me. I do not know why. Perhaps the old gods were angry that we had left them, and perhaps the Christian God was angry because we did not come sooner,—you know my people were among the last to follow the new religion,—and perhaps the new God was not pleased that I still kept the rune on my sword. I do not know, but the sword broke, and I was carried to the Danish camp, a captive. I struck down one of my captors, and the others said that it was a brave deed, and that my life should be spared, and that I should feast with them. While they drank, I sang to them. I was wild in my agony; my only thought was revenge. I sang, I jested, I made their orgies last as long as I could, that they might be the more wearied and sleep the more heavily."

"And then you cut your way out?" said the other.

"Yes, but that was not so hard as the waiting. At last one after another had fallen asleep. Even the sentinels were stupefied. I grasped the nearest sword. Heathen or not, this sword did not fail me. I have avenged my people."

"That was many years ago?" asked his friend.

"Yes, twelve or thirteen. My little son would have been a man, and would have stood by my side, should they come again. Here, where you see these two high mounds, they fought, the heathen and the Saxons. I have seen red blood trickle over the edge of that cliff," and as he gazed absently at the mound, his eyes grew dim, and he was forgetful of all but the past.

Almost as absently his companion looked out over the water. He started. "Eardwulf," he said, "my eyes are younger than yours, but yours can see a Dane farther than those of any other man. Is that a cloud or a Danish fleet?"

In a moment Eardwulf was an eager warrior.

"It is the Danes," he cried. "They may be coming here. Kindle the wood that is on top of the mound. Throw on damp moss and make a smoke. Our people will see it and prepare as best they can to defend themselves. We will make our way to the boats and be with them as soon as may be to help them. Oh, I could meet the whole army alone!"

The fleet came nearer and nearer. The people of Kent were aroused to their danger. They did what they could to fortify their homes, and many sought refuge in the cathedral at Canterbury, only partially rebuilt since its previous sack by the Danes. Men were on every hill that commanded a view of the sea, watching anxiously the approach of the foe. Women caught up their children and clasped them in what they feared might be almost a last embrace.

Nearer and nearer came the fleet. It sailed past the white cliffs of Thanet, south, west. The Saxons nearest the shore could see the dreaded flag of the pirates. They could hear the wild shouts and songs of their foes. From the column of smoke the Danes had guessed that their arrival was known, and they had no care to keep silence. Around the southern coast of Thanet they sailed. The Saxons trembled, as they seemed to hesitate for a moment. Then the boats were turned toward the island. The Danes sprang ashore. From the careful way in which they moored their vessels, the Saxons reasoned that there would be no immediate attack, and they were grateful for even a small respite.

Word had been sent to King Ethelbert, and he and his counselors were discussing what was best to do. Eardwulf, the noble thegn who had begged to be permitted to act as coast guard that he might be the first to see the enemy, had been sent to the king to beg for his aid and protection. Alstan, the warrior bishop, was there, though so feeble that he had to be helped into the room. He was an old man, but his dark eyes were as fiery as ever, and his voice was clear and strong. He was seated in a great arm-chair with a high carved back. Much against his will, a footstool had been brought, and cushions had been piled around him. Ethelbert sat in the middle of the royal seat, and on either side of him were the princes, Ethelred and Alfred. The high back of the throne was draped with a rich purple silk, whose edges were embroidered with a heavy tracery of gold, flashing here and there with amethysts. The walls of the room were draped with dark red cloth, a necessary precaution in those days when even kings' palaces were full of draughts. In an irregular half-circle around the sons of Ethelwulf were the trusted counselors of the king, though Eardwulf's impatience would not allow him to sit quietly, and every few minutes he would leave his seat and pace restlessly back and forth in front of the dais.

"You have heard the story of Eardwulf," said the king. "Do you advise that we do as he urges, march straightway to the eastern coast and attack the Danes on the island?"

"I have seen the water that lies between Thanet and the mainland red with blood, and it was not all the blood of the heathen," said one.

"The Danes are few; they do not expect a night attack. We could surprise them, and when morning came, their dead bodies would have been thrown over the cliffs," said another.

Ethelred nodded acquiescence. Ethelwulf looked serious and thoughtful. Alfred was intently listening, bending forward to catch every word of the speaker. Ethelred was crown prince, and it was not customary to permit a second heir to the throne to have any share in the deliberations of the king's council; but Alfred, though he was not yet sixteen, had inspired far more respect than his years would seem to warrant. He could read and write, he had made a pilgrimage to Rome and had been blessed by the Pope and anointed with the holy oil. Ethelbert held the kingdom in trust for his younger brothers, and Ethelred had manifested so little interest in the affairs of state that some had begun to feel that it would be wise to pass him by in the succession to the throne, and to hope that he would of his own accord retire to a convent before any question of his accession should arise. Alfred had already shown his bravery and his good judgment, and the chief anxiety felt on his account was lest his health should fail, for it was known that he was afflicted with some painful disease that no one understood. No wonder that more than one of the gray-haired counselors watched with intense interest to see what the boy would say.

"His blue eyes are as keen as Alstan's black ones," whispered one.

"Yes," said another; "but do you see how his lips tremble when the pain comes to him?"

"If they would only bleed him and give him saffron," whispered the first. "That is good for the lungs and the liver and the eyes and the stomach and—" but the king was speaking.

"Ethelred," he said, "do you advise waiting to see what the Danes will do?"

"Yes," said Ethelred. "If they do no harm to us, why should we attack them?" Eardwulf stopped short in his walk and looked upon the heir to the throne with but half-concealed scorn. Then he turned eagerly to the younger prince.

"Ought the men of Wessex to leave their own land?" said Alfred. "Is there not danger of raids by the heathen on our own coast?" Eardwulf's face fell, and he involuntarily grasped his sword; but the prince went on as simply as if he was thinking aloud.

"Would it not be well before they offer any harm to try to make peace with them, to gain time to train our men, and to bring together so many of them that part could defend Wessex and part be ready to help the men of Kent?"

The keen, piercing eyes of Alstan were fixed upon the face of the youth, and now in response to a look from the king, he spoke, rising slowly and painfully to his feet and leaning on the back of the great chair.

"King Ethelbert," he said, "to my mind the voice of the youngest at the council advises well. We are not strong enough, alas, to make a successful attack upon the Danes and to defend our own land of Wessex at the same time, should need arise. Let us, then, make a treaty with our foes, that they may some day be glad to beg for a treaty with us; and let us teach and train our men so that workingmen who have never borne a sword may know how to wield one, and drive the heathen from our land forever. Let us make all men see that he who oppresses one man oppresses all; then, and then alone, can we hope to become free. What is your will, O king?"

"When the voice of the oldest and of the youngest are as one, the king must agree," said Ethelbert. "I think that you are right. We will try to make the treaty, and we will train the men. Eardwulf, my noble thegn," he added, "do not be so downcast. The day of reckoning is not past. It will surely come. We but delay it a little that it may be the more crushing."

Eardwulf was but half satisfied, but he returned to Kent to report the king's will. A treaty was made with the Danes, by which they promised to do no harm to the Saxons. The Saxons gave them a great weight of silver, and promised them an equal amount of gold if the men of Kent were unmolested during the winter.

All knew that little confidence could be placed in the word of the Danes, and a close watch was kept of their movements. At first they seemed undecided what to do. Almost every day they would go out with their boats. If they sailed to the south, the men of Kent would tremble; if to the north, there was joy, for there was always hope that they would not return. Sometimes they would sail past Essex or even as far as the coast of East Anglia; and everywhere men would send their women and children into hiding, and grasp their spears and swords and battle-axes, and stand ready to meet the dreaded heathen. Once they sailed into the mouth of the Thames, and fleet horsemen galloped to give warning to London; but the invaders landed on the island of Sheppey, and remained there for several days, as harmless as any company of picnickers; but wherever they went there was fear. Some thought that this landing on Sheppey might signify that they would spend the winter on one island or the other, and recalled the fact that some ten years previously a band of Danes had wintered on Sheppey and had done little damage to their unwilling neighbors.

At last they seemed to have settled down for the winter. They put up a rude shelter for their boats, and even built some rough, half-open huts of branches of trees with a clumsy thatching of twigs and rushes and seaweed.

The few boats that were left unprotected and ready for use were rather of the heavier, more substantial kind than the light skiffs with which they could so easily glide up even the most shallow streams or land on low-lying shores.

These were better adapted to deep-sea fishing, and when the Saxons found that they seemed to be taken out only at such times as it would be necessary to provide food, the long-suffering people began to breathe more freely, even though the blazing campfires that shone out at night on the high land of Thanet were a continual threat and menace.

Meanwhile King Ethelbert was not idle. Each ealderman could call out all the free men of his district to form a fighting force. They could fight, but they had little training for battle. Indeed, a regular battle was a thing almost unheard of. Thus far the attacks of the Danes had almost always been sudden and upon small bodies. They would glide up the rivers in their boats, or they would land at some distant point and make their way through the wilderness as silently as the snake, and in the early gray of the morning pounce down upon the sleeping men; or they would come just before the sunset, when men were scattered in the fields and wearied with the labors of the day, and the women were alone in their homes preparing the evening meal. They were always expected, and their coming was always unexpected. To oppose this kind of attack, regular drill would count for little. The first thing to be done was to provide plenty of weapons and practise as many men in their use as possible.

Naturally enough, men were unwilling to leave their own homes where they might be needed at any moment in order to defend other parts of the country; and this feeling was the stronger from the fact that travel, even from one shire to another, was not common. Where a man was born, that was his place. There was his land, his home. If he was well, the lord of his district must give him work and protect him; if he was sick, his lord must care for him. If he left his home, there was nothing for him to do, and nowhere for him to go. Every one of the great farms had men enough to cultivate it. There were no manufactures; little work of any kind could be found. The man who abandoned his home had neither work, food, nor protection. He must starve or become a vagabond and robber. Kent and Wessex were nominally one kingdom, but with such difficulties as these in the way of sending men from the west to help men of the east, the experience of Alstan and the wise instinct of Alfred had both pointed to the only course open to them, to try to make a treaty to gain time in the hope that things would change for the better.

The smiths were busy. Night and day the forges were ablaze, and swords, axes, spearheads, arrowheads, and coats of mail were made in great numbers. Following the example of the king, men practised athletic exercises, and skilled themselves in the use of arms as they had never done before. What this might have accomplished we do not know, for before the spring came, the blow fell.

A winter of so complete inactivity was a thing almost unknown to the Danes. Cramped up on the little island of Thanet, they grew wild and restless.

"This is no life for a sea king," said one of them, "to gather rushes for the roof and wood for the camp-fire. Bah! One might as well be a Saxon."

"My brother stays at home to care for the inheritance," said another. "My country is the sea. The land is for our plunder, not to live on."

"And just across the water is the fair country of Kent. We can see the high towers of the churches, and—"

"And that is where the priests and monks live, and where they make charms against us," broke in another. "Who knows whether we shall be able to go from the island or not? They have magic, these priests, in their books, and they may bewitch our vessels so that they will float before their eyes, helpless forever, and we ourselves be fixed as firmly to the island as that white cliff."

"The blood of my father trickled over that cliff," said another, "and I catch fish and sleep under a roof while he is unavenged!"

"If we wait till spring, they will give us gold," said one, thoughtfully.

"And where will their gold come from?" demanded another indignantly. "From their churches and their convents. There they are before us. The land lies open. The gold is there. Shall the sons of Odin and Thor wait for what their swords will give them until it is the pleasure of these puny islanders to say, 'You may have it'? We do not give gifts to our little children in that way. We say, 'Take it, and if another child is the stronger, let him take it from you if he can.' The sword of the Danes is the will of the gods."

The camp-fires were built up brighter than ever, that the Saxons might not suspect their plans, and in a fiendish glee the Danes went to the moorings, but as softly as if their steps could be heard on the opposite shore where the Saxons lay sleeping. Without a sound the boats were made free, and soon the invaders were on the other side and gliding softly up the river Stour. For some reason they did not go as far as Canterbury. Perhaps they were too jubilant in their new liberty to unite in anything like an organized attack upon a larger place, but they ran through eastern Kent like a whirlwind of fire, bursting down upon the smaller villages with all the horrors of a midnight onslaught, tearing down the wooden churches, seizing the treasures, and setting fire to the ruins. It was like a mad frolic of fiends. They sought gold and silver, but for the joys of bloodshed and torture they would gleefully turn aside from the richest treasure. Blood rather than gold was their delight; they were ravenous beasts, not men, and they reveled in the agonies of their victims.

Before the morning came, they had departed. Those that had survived the terrors of the night were too full of suffering and too sick at heart to question whither.

When the news of the massacre and the ravaging of the country of Kent was brought to the king, he turned pale, but said not one word; and his efforts were redoubled to make his men better and better prepared for battle.

"The day of revenge will come, King Ethelbert," said one of his thegns.

"It is not revenge," answered the king, sternly, "it is not revenge. The day for revenge is past. It is for freedom, not revenge, that we must fight. The murderers must be driven from our shores. On the sea they are greater than we; but they must be made to fear to step on Saxon soil."

"But they have gone," said Ethelred. "Why do you work so hard to make ready to fight against them? Perhaps they will never come back."

The king turned away wearily, and answered nothing.

Chapter XI.
"I Must Serve My People"

When Alfred was told of the massacre, he was cut to the heart. "It is my own men of Kent," he said. "If I could only have been with them!" Then he remembered and understood Swithin's lament when Winchester was sacked and burned, "My people, O my people!" "What can I do for my people?" the boy questioned. The thought pressed too heavily upon him. He could not be still; he must go somewhere, do something. A company was just starting for the woods to hunt; he caught up a spear and galloped after them.

It was not safe to go any distance into the forest alone, but before long Alfred had left his companions far behind him. On and on he rode. Deer sprang away before him, but his bow hung idle. Wolves howled faintly in the distance, only waiting for twilight to make their attack, but he did not even grasp his sword the more firmly. Faster and faster he went, realizing nothing of his whereabouts until between the trees he caught a glimpse of a little village. He was in no mood to meet people and receive the homage that they would pay him as their favorite prince. He checked his horse and sought a roundabout way to avoid the villagers. Only one did he meet, and that one far from the houses, an old woman wandering aimlessly about. She was bent and bowed and almost blind, but worse than all that, Alfred saw at a glance that she was afflicted with all the horrors of leprosy. The sickly white of her skin, the ghastly ravages of the disease—it was more than the young prince in his highly excited mood could bear. He spurred his horse and went on faster than ever.

"To be like that," he gasped, "to be a horror and a dread to my people! I could not bear it. Anything but that! The pain is nothing." But even as he spoke, the suffering of the disease that no one could understand or lessen came suddenly upon him. He slipped from his horse and lay on the ground only half conscious, but saying to himself over and over again:—

"Anything but that, anything but that!"

The pain disappeared as suddenly as it came, and he looked around him. He was alone. His horse was quietly feeding near by and came at his call. He was on the outskirts of the village. Not far away, at the edge of the rocky valley, was a tiny church, and into it Alfred made his way, staggering from weakness. A single priest was at the altar. The prince knelt reverently. When the prayer was over, he approached the priest.

"I am Alfred the prince," he said. "Will you send some one to care for my horse, and will you leave me here all night? I must be alone." The priest bent low before him.

"The blessing of the church be upon you, and the God of the church be with you," he said as he closed the door. The prince was alone. He flung himself before the altar.

"Anything but that," he prayed, "anything but that! My people would scorn me. I must serve my people. Any pain, any suffering, but let me help my people. Give me strength. Give me wisdom, not for myself, but for my people."

Long the prince pleaded; then he slept, soundly and sweetly, even on the hard floor before the altar.

It was morning when he awoke. The day was bright and sunny. His heart was at rest. He knew not what lay before him, but he believed that his prayer would be answered. In that night Alfred had left his boyhood behind him. He was a man, and the cares and burdens of a man were pressing nearer to him than he knew.

He rode slowly through the forest, breathing in the freshness of the early morning, stopping for a moment to enjoy the plashing and gurgling of every tiny brook, seeing every ray of sunlight that beamed softly down through the branches upon a bed of green moss, or brought out the rich golden brown of some pool lying sleepily under the trees. He felt himself a man. He knew that dangers and responsibilities lay before him, but he felt strong to encounter them.

As he rode up to the palace, his brother met him.

"I have been a little anxious about you, Alfred," he said. "It is not your wont to stay away so long."

"No, it is not," said Alfred. "I will not do it again. I did not remember that you might be alarmed," and, indeed, he had felt so full of responsibility that he had forgotten that any one might feel responsible for him.

"I was in the little village far to the west of us," he said. "I spent the night alone in the church." The king looked a little troubled but he said only:—

"Bishop Alstan has been asking for you. He wishes to see you."

"He is not ill?" asked the prince quickly.

"No, but he is very feeble. We cannot hope to have him with us long. He has done his work nobly and rest is good. Rest is good," repeated the king a little wearily, and as Alfred looked at him, he was struck by the worn look on his pale face.

"You are tired," he said. "I wish that I could help you."

"You do help me," said the king, laying his hand on the

prince's shoulder, "and the thought of you rests me. It will make it easier to lay down the heavy burden when the time of freedom comes. But now go and find the bishop."

Alfred rode away a little saddened, but feeling himself even more of a man because of his older brother's trust and his rare words of affectionate confidence.

It was not the way of the soldier bishop to make long preambles to what he had to say, and after a brief welcome he began:—

"I have known your brothers, your father, and your grandfather. I have watched the sons of Ethelwulf from their childhood. King Ethelbert will not have a long life; the feeble old bishop may live longer than he. Where will the kingdom fall? Into the hands of Ethelred, trembling and uncertain as they are. I could overthrow his claims even now. Weak and worn as I am, there are strong arms ready to do my bidding; but to thrust him from the throne would be to arouse a party in his favor, and the kingdom must not be divided. No, it is best that he should be king, but the real power must rest in your hands. Do you fear to accept it?"

"I will do the best that I can for my people. What is for their good shall ever be first with me," said the prince solemnly.

"That is good," said the old man, gazing keenly into the eyes of the youth. "I believe that you will keep your word. There is a new manliness in your face, a something that I have not seen there before. You are a boy in years, but you have the heart of a man and some of the man's wisdom."

"I am enough of a man to value your advice," said Alfred. "If I should ever—if the time comes of which you speak, what ought I to do?"

"First of all," said the bishop in a low, clear voice, "you must demand of Ethelred your share of the property left by your father. If he yields it to you, matters will be easier; but I think he will not yield. He has a vague idea that in some way, if he only holds on to it, he can give more to the church. That one thought is firmly fixed in his mind, and he will not understand that to give even to the church money and lands that belong to another will bring no blessing. If he refuses, you can do no more, for you must stand together. It is a difficult position for even a man of experience. You must be the power in the kingdom, but you must act only as your brother's agent, or at least seem to do so.

"There is one word more. I have been something of a soldier in my time. There will be fighting in our land, worse than has ever been before. When our people came, they drove the Britons to the westward till they took refuge in the wildest mountain fastnesses of Wales; and I have feared lest the Danes in time soon to come drive us too from our homes to some other place, perhaps across the water to the land that is beyond the country of the Cambrians. Now that my arm is feeble, I see what we need. All that will save us is union. Two men together have the strength of three separately, but we are separated. When Kent is ravaged, we are glad it is not Wessex; and when Winchester is sacked, the men of Kent rejoice that they have escaped. That has been our mistake. You must try to make each division of your kingdom feel that what hurts any one part hurts all. Unite, if you would save your country. Unite, if you would have a country to save." The old man sank back wearied. The prince bent low and kissed his hand in farewell.

"My bishop and my soldier," he said, "of all that has been said to me I will take heed."

"The boy has the mind of a man," murmured the bishop, "for he can listen; and he has the heart of a king, for he can obey. The land is safe in his hands. Mine eyes have seen its salvation. I may depart in peace."

Ethelbert worked with a feverish eagerness to prepare his men for fighting. Night and day the forges were aglow, and at any hour the king was likely to come in upon the workmen and even to take a hand in the work himself to teach them some better way that he had learned or invented.

Ethelred paid little attention to the preparations that were going on around him. The Danes were not in sight, why then fear their coming? Perhaps they would not come at all. So he reasoned, and went on with his usual occupations, while Alfred was taking his place in aiding the king in his efforts. He had gained much that was of practical value from his reading, and he was quick to see the better way of doing a thing. The king was most grateful for the help and interest of his younger brother. He worked more eagerly than ever, till one day his over-tasked strength gave way. There was no disease, or at least none that the primitive medical skill of the time could discover. He simply grew weaker day by day, and it was not long before he, too, was laid in Sherborne Cathedral.

The grief throughout the land was most sincere, for Ethelbert was loved and respected; and while Ethelred had no enemies, all who came near him had learned to fear his weakness in important matters and his occasional obstinacy in trifles. Many looked upon the younger brother, and wished that he, even with his lack of years and of experience, might be placed upon the throne. This feeling went no further than words, however, both because Alstan's wishes were powerful among them, and because even the most restless feared the trouble that would follow division and rivalry. Yet it is hard to say what might have been the result, had not Alfred invariably discouraged any suggestion that he should take the first place. Whatever he did, he did in the name of Ethelred. "My brother, the king," was always his authority.

But the time had come when, if he obeyed the words of Alstan, he must formally demand his share of the inheritance. It must be in the presence of the king's council, and there it was that with nobles and thegns looking on he laid his claim before the king.

"King Ethelred, my brother," he said, "it is now six years since you and I willingly laid our possessions into the hand of Ethelbert that his stronger arm might guard them for us. They have now passed into your hands. It is right that I should receive what my father wished me to have; and it is only fitting that the crown prince should have lands and treasures of his own that he may the better learn to care for the larger interests that may one day come to him. I ask you for my share of the possessions left by my father."

The counselors nodded their approval, and the keen eyes of Alstan fairly shone with pleasure at the quiet dignity of the young prince's speech.

In great contrast with this was the somewhat confused reply of Ethelred. It was to the effect that some of the property had come directly from their father, some through Ethelbald and Ethelbert; that some lay in Wessex, some in Kent; that there had been changes in value because of the ravages of the Danes; that some of it was to be divided between them, while some belonged to himself alone; and that if Alfred would be content until his death, he would then leave all to him, both what belonged to them jointly and any that he, Ethelred, might afterward acquire.

The counselors looked grave. Here and there one involuntarily put his hand on his sword. There was a murmur of disapproval, but here and there was an answering murmur of satisfaction.

"The prince should have his own," whispered one.

"Better that it should stay in one man's hands," said another.

"The prince would give its revenues for the defense of the kingdom—" but Ethelred was asking the formal question:—

"Are you content?" and Alfred with one glance at the varying expressions on the faces of the counselors before him, said quietly:—

"I am content."

Wise, indeed, was Alstan in counseling peace and union between the two brothers, whatever might betide, for never was there a time when variance between members of the royal family would have wrought more of harm to the Saxons. Up to this time the Danish invaders had been roving bands of marauders, cruel because their nature and training led to cruelty, but with no special determination to torture and to kill. They burned and demolished with no particular malice toward the owners of the land that they ravaged and the property that they destroyed, but simply because they felt a fiendish delight in destruction and ruin. An invasion of a far different nature was soon to take place, one that would require all Ethelbald's strengthening of defenses, all Ethelbert's making of weapons and training of men, and all of Alfred's young strength together with a wisdom far beyond his years, before the island should become in reality England, Angleland, the land of the Angles.

For many years the name most feared by the men of northeastern England was that of Ragnar Lodbrog. He was no common marauder. His mother was a Danish princess, his father a Norwegian of high rank. He himself had sat on the throne of the Danish islands. A rival king had driven him from his kingdom, but soon had to beg for aid from the Franks against Lodbrog's increasing power, for the deposed king was worshiped by the island chieftains who had become his followers.

They had reason to look up to him. He was a king; his mother had been of royal birth; his father had risen to the highest position by his own merits. He was a man of talent, and this talent was not wholly uncultivated. Of all the Baltic countries, Denmark was nearest the Frankish kingdom, and he had received as much education as his wild nature could accept. When he set forth, therefore, on his career of piracy, his name carried with it a certain repute that attracted to him the boldest of the nobles; and it was not long before the sound of that name would make men tremble, not only on the shores of the Baltic and in England, but also in France, and perhaps even on the Mediterranean coasts.

He was a plunderer and a robber, but plundering and robbery were regarded by the Danes as a noble occupation. To stay at home, to live on the treasure of one's fathers, that was humiliation, and the son that was chosen to be the heir was looked upon with a certain pity. To go out upon the ocean and fight one's way with the sword, that was honor, that was worthy of a man descended even from the great gods themselves.

Most of the other Danish pirates gave themselves with a reckless confidence to the chances of the sea, landing wherever the winds and the waves bore them; but the exploits of Lodbrog gained a certain dignity from the fact that his invasions always had a definite object, that he set out on no journey without a definite destination. In revenge for the aid that the Franks had given to his rival, he sailed up the Seine to destroy Paris. The people heard of his coming and fled in terror. He began to demolish the city, but after he had torn down one monastery, the king bribed him with a gift of seven thousand pounds to depart.

The scene of his next exploits was to be the British islands. He was successful in ravaging parts of Scotland and Ireland; and now he planned a greater expedition than any one before him had undertaken. He would land on the coast of Northumbria, rich in convents with their accumulated treasures, and he would bring home such a load of gold and silver and jewels as never boat had carried before.

He built two great vessels, larger than any that had ever been seen in the Danish waters. From far and near, people came to look upon the wonderful things, and to predict the mighty deeds that would be done in the land of the Angles. Nobles and chieftains begged for a chance to go with him who had become the pride of their land. He might easily have been made their king if he had chosen, but he scorned the land save as a repository for his treasure; his kingdom was the sea.

The bravest men of Denmark were suppliants before him; he had only to choose. The night before they set sail there was a great feast. Bonfires blazed and flashed their light from island to island, until the narrow straits glowed with the reflection of the flame. Songs of heroes and of gods were chanted, war-poems "with a sword in every line." Last of all came the song that they believed was written by Odin himself:—

> "Cattle die,
> Kindred die,
> We ourselves also die;
> But the fair fame never dies
> Of him who has earned it."
>
> *Thorpe's translation.*

The day of their starting was wild and stormy, just such a time as the Danish pirates liked; and exulting as if the victory was already won, they passed out into the North Sea. The wind was from the east, and they had an almost straight course. All went well until they were near the land; then came conflicting winds and currents. With their light boats, they would have been at ease, but they knew nothing of navigating the unwieldy monsters that had been the pride of the Danish land. The vessels were wrecked, and they were thrown helpless upon the coast of their enemies.

In a free combat the Danes had, man for man, no superiority over the Saxons. Danish victories had been due to the quickness of their movements, to the unexpectedness of their arrivals, and to their rapidity in striking a sudden blow and then retreating before their opponents could gather together. In this instance, there was warning of their approach; they could not move so rapidly as the Saxons who knew the ground, and they had no way of retreating. It was hopeless from the first, but the proud king would not beg for mercy, and he could hardly have expected to receive it, if he had humbled himself to ask it.

Ella, king of Deira, marched against him. There was a fierce combat, for the Danes fought like men who must put all their force into one blow, and the Saxons like men who had but one chance to avenge the most bitter wrongs. Four times Lodbrog dashed through the lines of Ella; four times he was thrust back. His friends were slain one by one, and he himself was captured. One could hardly expect King Ella to be magnanimous, but the death that he decreed for his royal prisoner, the idol of Denmark, was to be thrown into a dungeon of vipers and to die in agony from their poison.

The old legend goes on to say that while Lodbrog was in Northumbria, his sons were winning victories in the south. They came home laden with treasure, and were quietly resting and making ready for another voyage when the tidings was brought them of their father's death. Two of the sons were playing chess, and they clutched the board till their hands bled. One had a knife in his hand, and he grasped the blade until, without knowing it, he had cut his fingers to the bone. One was polishing his spear, and his fingers left their impress on the hard iron. These four made the most terrible threats of vengeance. Inguar, the eldest, said nothing, but his face was fearful to look upon. In some way the scene was reported to King Ella. He smiled until the look of Inguar was described; then he trembled and said:—

"It is Inguar or no one that I fear."

Chapter XII.

THE COMING OF THE SONS OF LODBROG

Silently the preparations of the Danes were made. The sons of Lodbrog went about from island to island, from coast to coast, rehearsing their father's fame, the glory that he had given to the north, and his fearful sufferings. Everywhere they found allies. Norway, Sweden, Denmark, Russia, all sent their bravest men. Every little village contributed its champion. Eight jarls, or earls, so the legends say, swore on their golden bracelets to avenge the death of the hero of the north. Perhaps no other country was ever so united in its wrath. The greatest of the vikings had been put to death; not slain in battle, but slaughtered contemptuously as a thing of naught. Men's rage was at a white heat. Rival chiefs forgot their enmity. Old feuds were laid aside. Men who hated each other clasped hands and vowed to avenge the dead leader as never man was avenged before. Many vessels were built, not heavy and large like those that had brought Lodbrog to his death, but light enough to be easily governed. The sons of Lodbrog took command, and over their war-ships floated the magic banner of the raven, made by Lodbrog's daughters in a single day.

Not a whisper of this was known in the land of the Saxons. Had Ethelbald been on the throne, his spies would have found out what was going on in the country across the sea; but the preparations began in the latter part of Ethelbert's reign, when he was too engrossed with his own preparations for resistance to give as close attention as he ought to what might have to be resisted; and so, when Ethelred came to the throne, the protection of England was left in the hands of a weak, irresolute king and a boy of seventeen, who had never seen a battle.

The Danes were a superstitious people, and before they would embark on any great undertaking, they always consulted their soothsayers. On an occasion of so much moment, everything was done with the utmost formality. The leaders of the expedition assembled in the hall of the noblest among them, although only nobles and men of high birth were present, for all humbler men had been excluded, and the hall purified by the burning of fragrant resins and spices. A large retinue of young men and maidens had been sent to attend the soothsayer and bring her to the hall. As she entered, the warriors beat their shields and flashed their naked swords three times around their heads in sign of welcome.

She was dressed in a long, trailing robe of dark green with many gold ornaments fastened on it. At the door, the owner of the hall met her and humbly proffered her his house and all that was his. She bowed slightly, and without a glance at him or at any of the rest of the company assembled before her, walked to the dais followed by her attendants, and sank upon a richly carved bench with high back, draped and cushioned with scarlet of the finest material that the maraudings of the Danes could furnish. Food was brought her, the most delicate that could be found, and prepared by the hands of the wife of the noble. She ate lightly and with no apparent consciousness of the many who were watching her movements.

The noble then approached her most reverently and begged that she would honor his poor house by prophesying; that when the morning came, she would of her great wisdom and goodness deign to predict what should be the success of himself and his friends in the mighty undertaking that they had in mind. The soothsayer gave a slight nod, and then all withdrew, leaving her alone in the hall.

All around the building there must be perfect silence or the charms would fail; but from a distance men watched, and through the crevices they saw strangely colored lights, and those that dared to come nearer heard weird chantings and shrill cries. Then the hall was still and dark; and then there were sounds like the tramping of many feet.

In the morning they waited patiently about the door. At last it opened and the soothsayer stood before them. She looked upon each one of them in turn. She smiled and said:—

"The hall is cleansed. No evil spirit remains within its walls to work you ill. Enter the door. Whatever you plan in this hall to-day shall be smiled upon by the gods. Naught shall resist you unless it be by the will of the fates, against whom the gods themselves are powerless."

Then the nobles flocked around her and begged her to accept their gifts, gold and silver bracelets and ornaments and rare furs and jewels. She smiled upon them once more and said:—

"Remember that the sword of the hero is the will of the gods. The fates alone can oppose you." Then she seated herself in the brightly painted wagon that had been brought for her, and was slowly driven away, while the men feasted and sang fierce songs of revenge and exultation.

The great fleet set sail and went straight to the coast of Northumbria. When they were not far from the land, a wind sprang up from the north.

"It is the breath of Thor," said one of the leaders. "He wills that we go to the southward."

"There is a wide harbor and a good landing-place for ships farther south," said one, "where a vessel would hardly rock with the touch of the waves in all the winter."

"Let us stay all winter," said another. "We are come for more than gold and silver. We are here for vengeance. Let us go home no more with a few loads of treasure; let us take the land itself. Let us stay all winter, and then when the warmer time has come, let us burn their monasteries and strike down their kings, and kill, kill, kill, and torture even as the mighty Lodbrog was tortured by these Christians—these traitors to Odin and to Thor. It is Thor whose breath fills our sails; he, too, would have revenge. Let us stay in the land to which he leads us."

There was a great shouting of approval, there were horrible cries of exultation and a deafening beating of the shields that made a grim bulwark to their vessels, when the word of their leaders was made known to them.

The fleet passed Northumbria and came to the shores of East Anglia. The boats were not large, but they were appalling. At their prows were figures of raging lions or wolves or savage bulls or a serpent might rear his frightful head over the waves that dashed against the ship. Many of the superstitions of the heathen were even yet in full force in the Saxon land. These Saxons were not cowards, but who could tell what awful fiends might be hidden under the cover of the form of a wild beast? No wonder that they feared when they thought that they might have to contend not only with their human foes, but with the demons that were their allies.

It was almost a relief when the pirates left their ships with a guard and marched inland; and when, instead of coming upon the Saxons with fire and sword, they went straight to the king's palace and demanded an audience, the people breathed more freely.

They really rejoiced when the invaders only demanded what they might easily have taken. A kind of treaty was made. The invaders agreed to winter quietly in their own lines along the shore, and to do no harm to the men of East Anglia. In return, their unwilling hosts were to furnish them with food and with horses.

There was no special reason for expecting the invaders to keep their part of the treaty, but the Saxons had no choice in the matter, and they could only wait, dreading what the spring would bring to them. The other Saxon states had little fear. The Danes had always landed where they meant to strike the first blow, and the Saxons had no idea that this invasion was in any respect different from the preceding ones.

When the first warm days of spring came, there was little need of questioning. More ships had arrived during the winter. Men swarmed like flies; the shore was black with them. With lowering brows the sons of Ragnar and their followers strode on, and as they marched, they burned and killed and tortured. Far to the northward they went, cutting through the helpless land a wide swath of ruin like the path of some malignant pestilence. At the river Tyne they halted, and turned to cut another terrible swath of devastation in their southward march.

There was almost no opposition, the country seemed paralyzed. Only union could save it, and Northumbria was torn by fierce dissension between Ella and Osbert, whom Ella had driven from the throne. At last the rivals united their forces. For once it was the Danes who were surprised; for when in their march to the south they came near the city of York, the Saxons dashed out from ambush and fell upon them. Great was their delight when the resistless Danes were forced to flee. In the northward march of the Danes they had partially destroyed the fortifications of York, and it was an easy matter for them to take refuge in the city.

If the Saxons had waited for reËnforcements, the whole course of the invaders might have been checked; but they were so little used to victory that, having once routed the heathen, they fancied themselves resistless, and madly tore down what remained of the city walls to get at their foes. They were only shutting themselves into a trap, for the Danes had recovered from their first surprise; they fell upon their enemies, and the whole Northumbrian army was cut down almost at a blow. Ella was taken alive, and was put to a lingering death with tortures too horrible to describe.

This was the beginning of the vengeance that the sons of Lodbrog visited upon the Saxons; but they were not yet satisfied, the whole land must be theirs. They took Northumbria for their rallying place. Stories of the riches of the island and the ease with which they might be won made their way back to the shores of the north. Relatives and friends of the leaders came in legions, until the narrow bounds of Northumbria would not contain them.

Meanwhile, the people of Wessex were comparatively free from danger, or thought they were, for they had at first no idea that the Danes meant anything more than a temporary invasion. The bonds between the different portions of the land were slight, although several of the weaker states were nominally tributary to Wessex; the more Northumbria suffered, the better were the chances of escape for the other countries. But fifteen years before, Buhred, the king of Mercia, had married King Ethelwulf's daughter Ethelswitha. These two kingdoms were adjoining, and this, together with the relationship between the rulers, had brought them into much closer intercourse than existed between either Northumbria or East Anglia and Wessex. More than once Buhred had bought off the Danes. If Mercia fell into their hands, Wessex would be the next to suffer. So Alfred reasoned, and at last it was decided that he should go to Mercia to visit his sister Ethelswitha and her husband Buhred, and to plan a closer union between Wessex and the tributary kingdom, should the need for defense arise.

In less than two months Alfred returned to report that Buhred did not think there was immediate danger of an invasion. He had made a kind of treaty with the Danes, and somehow, even after all their sad experience, it never seemed to occur to the Saxons that their heathen foes could break their word. Perhaps Alfred's eyes were not so keen in looking for Danes as they should have been, for they were bent upon one Lady Elswitha, daughter of a princess of the royal family and one of the most revered nobles of Mercia. Alfred was not yet twenty, but this was not an unusually youthful age for marriage; moreover, it was regarded as ungallant to postpone the wedding ceremony many weeks after the betrothal.

Being married was in those days a somewhat complicated proceeding. First came the solemn betrothal, the promise of the groom to the bride's nearest male relative that he would care for her as a man ought to care for the one who is dearest to him. The promise alone was not enough, for he had to bring forward men as his security who must forfeit a large sum if he did not keep his word. He must then name the gift that he would present to her for agreeing to be his wife, and what he would give her if she lived longer than he. After this, the bride's father pronounced the words:—

"I give thee my daughter to be thy honor and thy wife."

All this took place at the house of the groom, whither the maiden had been brought with great ceremony. Her future husband had gone with his friends in search of her. They were armed, lest any former lover should pursue and try to steal her from them. The bride's father and brothers, indeed all her male relatives, escorted her, and a company of her girl friends went with her as bridesmaids.

The marriage ceremony was performed in the church. Both bride and groom were crowned with flowers, and it was partly because of the lavish use of flowers that the usual time of celebrating marriages was the summer.

Then came the wedding feast. All day, all night, far into the next day, the festivities went on; for at the wedding of a prince, what limit could be put to the rejoicing? The men of Mercia were happy, for was it not yet another bond between their land and the stronger land of Wessex? Why need they fear the heathen army when the soldiers of Wessex would be ready to aid them in repelling their foes? The men of Wessex rejoiced none the less, for it was the wedding of their beloved prince, of him who would one day be their king. As the feast went on, they talked of his prowess in hunting, how he was ever first in the chase, how little he seemed to care for danger or fatigue.

"And even as a little child, he made the great pilgrimage," said one, "and he remembers still just where the Pope touched him with the holy oil."

"The Lady Elswitha comes of the royal line," said another, looking at the head of the long table where the royal pair were seated. "Her father is the wisest of King Buhred's counselors; and her mother is a noble woman, she has been almost as a mother to Queen Ethelswitha since she became the wife of King Buhred."

"Do you remember Queen Osburga, the mother of Ethelswitha?" asked one.

"Yes," said his neighbor, "and I stood nearest to her when the prince was starting out on his journey to Rome. I saw her kiss the jewel at his neck, and I heard her words. She said that in time to come he would lose it, but he must not mourn, for then his hardest days would be past; and she pointed to the southwest. She spoke like a soothsayer. Could it be that she meant the time when he spent a day and a night alone in the chapel at Cornwall? That lies far to the southwest—but no, for he still wears the jewel about his neck. That night the priest did not dare to leave him. He said that the fiends sometimes harassed a good man even in a church, and so he lay all night under the window to guard the prince."

"And did any fiend appear?"

"No, but he closed his eyes once for a moment, and he says that as he opened them, he is almost sure that he saw a bright light. Saint Guerir is buried there, and it might have been over his grave, and perhaps this was why evil spirits dared not come near. He heard the prince praying before the altar. He thinks he was begging to be freed from his disease, for he heard him say, 'Anything but that,' but he could not understand all."

"The trouble has nearly left him, has it not?"

"Yes, it is long since he has been troubled by it. They say that if one makes the pilgrimage to Rome, he may ask what he will."

The feasting went on. All the luxury of the two kingdoms had been brought together to do honor to the beloved prince and his bride. The hall was hung with bright scarlet draperies embroidered with figures of men and horses, representing the early battles of the Saxons with the Britons. The tables at which they feasted were richly carved and inlaid in graceful designs with silver and mother of pearl. They were almost too beautiful to be covered as they were, even with the cloths of fair white linen. The royal seats were inlaid with ivory and gold, and draped with purple bordered with golden fringes. There were great cups of gold and of silver; and when all had well eaten and drunk, there came in troops of tumblers and dancers and jugglers and men with trained animals. Then came the songs of the harpers, the wild chantings of the deeds of their ancestors, of the stabbing of monsters of the sea, of fire-breathing dragons whose many heads were cut off at a single blow by a wonderful sword: of the half-wild Britons whom they found in the island and drove to the westward; and then the strain grew more gentle, and they sang softly of the little child who had grown up among them to be their prince, and who would one day become their king. Alfred smiled and half shook his head as the music changed again and the harpers sang of the fair-haired boy who had pursued the wild boar, and had slain him on his first hunt; but the feasters only cheered and shouted louder and louder. Then they sang of the noble maiden who had become the bride of their prince, and of the joy of the two lands in the alliance.

The great hall resounded with their shouts, the merriment was at its height; but in a moment every voice was hushed, and men sprang to their feet and grasped their swords, or turned instinctively to their spears leaning in martial clusters against the wall. What was it? Would they have to fight with men or with fends? Was it a wile of Satan? Was it poison? The prince in the very fulness of his happiness had given a deep groan and fallen forward heavily to the floor.

" 'Tis his old infirmity come upon him again," whispered one.

"No," said another; "that did not come in this way. Some one has bewitched him."

"But he has not an enemy in the kingdom."

"They say the heathen have great power in magic, and that if they stick a thorn into an image of wax and melt it before a fire, and say over it a man's name, the man will die. Perhaps this is the work of Satan himself," and he made the sign of the cross.

"It is an unlucky day," said one. "The wedding should have been yesterday or to-morrow. To-day the moon is just five days old, and what is begun to-day will not be finished."

Men skilled in leechcraft were present, but all their remedies were tried in vain. Gradually the prince came to himself, but the pain lasted till nightfall; and ever after this time, for many years, the mysterious illness would come upon him with its agonies. No one could predict the attack, and the prince upon whose shoulders a nation's need was to press so heavily was never free from either intense pain or the dread of its coming. Between the attacks, however, it seemed to have little effect upon his health and strength.

The suffering passed, and Alfred and his bride went in joyful procession to the land of the West Saxons. A long train of wagons bore the wedding gifts, silver and golden dishes, silver mirrors, candlesticks, bracelets, earrings, and brooches, all set with precious stones, and garments of silk and of fine wool. There were tables and benches and high-backed chairs carved into figures of flowers and animals. There were low bedsteads, bed-curtains, and coverlets, and everything was of the richest description and most beautifully ornamented, for was it not the day of rejoicing of their beloved prince? Nothing that was in their power to obtain was too costly to give him.

There were musicians, too, in the retinue, and as they went on happily, there were jubilant sounds of flutes and trumpets and horns and drums and cymbals.

It was a time of happiness, a flash of joy in the night of gloom that was to fall upon the land of the Saxons. For one blissful hour the people forgot the sufferings that lay behind them, and had no thought of what might be before them. Joyfully, then, Alfred carried his bride to her new home, but almost before the long train of wagons had been unloaded, the fleetest of messengers came from Buhred.

"Help me; the Danes are upon me!"

Chapter XIII.

THE DANES AT CROYLAND

Now was the time to show the value of Ethelbert's making of arms and training of men. The fighting men of Wessex were far better prepared than ever before, and many who had never been called on to bear arms were now filled with a great desire to engage in battle for the first time. Some of them had lost their homes by the onslaughts of the Danes in previous years. The wives of some had been carried away into Danish slavery, and the children put to death with the cruelties of savages. Never was there an army more zealous to fight or more sure of victory.

The Northmen had come in such numbers that the narrow boundaries of Northumbria were too confined for them. Food was giving out, and the harvest was still several months distant. The vikings were growing restless, others were coming, they must have food, battle, conquest. Down the "wide vale of Trent" they swept, under the oaks of Sherwood Forest, devastating the land like a swarm of locusts; and yet so swiftly, so silently did they move that almost before the Saxons had begun their enthusiastic march, they were in the very heart of the Mercian kingdom and safely entrenched behind the strong gray walls of Nottingham.

The forces of Wessex and of Mercia pressed on eagerly to the city; but there before them stood the stronghold perched on its precipitous cliffs. They had hoped to intercept the enemy before they reached so safe a retreat, but they were too late. The walls rose before them as frowningly as if they had been the work of the Danes; and over the top peered the mocking faces of their foes, jeering at them and calling on them to come and take back their city if they wanted it.

To the weapons of the Saxons the walls were impregnable; they could not enter the city. The Danes had never met in direct fight so great and apparently so well-trained a force of Saxons; they dared not come out. So matters rested for many days.

"If we only had Alstan to advise us!" said the king; but Alstan had died the year before. His attendant had found the warrior bishop dead, sitting upright in his chair, and looking calmly straight before him. He had met death like a Christian soldier, trustfully and fearlessly.

A commander of far more experience than Alstan might well have hesitated to advise in this case. To leave the enemy safely fortified behind the city walls was to have accomplished nothing; but Danish reËnforcements might come at any moment, and worse than this, the Saxon soldiers were becoming restless. They had been eager to fight, but to settle down in inaction and spend their time gazing at an enemy who were as secure as if in Denmark, and whose uproarious feasting might be heard night after night, this was quite another matter. It is hardly a wonder that they grumbled among themselves.

"Ethelbald would have known what to do," said one soldier.

"The heathen killed my wife. This is what I want to do," said another, and he swung his sword around fiercely. "I want to kill a Dane for every hair on her head, not to sit here while they jeer at me." And in another group they were saying:—

"It is time for the harvest, and there is hardly a man in our district to reap the grain. The crop will not be large this year at best, and if we are starving, the convents cannot help us, for the monks and the priests have come with us to fight, and there is no one to reap their fields."

The Northmen, on the other hand, dwelling in safety behind the thick walls of Nottingham, were by no means at ease. ReËnforcements might come, to be sure, but they knew nothing of the abilities of the Saxons with an army so carefully prepared for war as this one seemed to be. Their noisy feasting and hilarious merriment were sometimes feigned for the purpose of deceiving their adversaries, for they were many and food was none too abundant in the beleaguered city.

No other way seems to have been open to either side than the one that they took. A parley was called. The Northmen agreed to return to Northumbria, and the Saxons promised to make no interference as they marched back with the booty which they had carried into Nottingham with them. The tiny stream of Idle was to be the line between the two peoples. It was hardly a glorious ending for Alfred's first campaign, but who can blame him or Ethelred, or suggest a wiser course of action?

One short year of respite had they from the fury of the north, and the poor, harassed land might have recovered herself and strengthened herself for a greater struggle, had it not been for a worse failure of the crops than any one had anticipated; and as if the famine was not enough, there came a pestilence upon the cattle, so that after a year of rest, the Saxon kingdoms were even less prepared than before to encounter the foe.

The year 870 was a hard year for the Saxons. Then, first, they began to realize that the Danes had other plans in mind than the gathering of booty, however rich, and sudden onslaughts, however fierce. Early in the autumn the enemy fell upon eastern Mercia. Its king made no effort to protect it; it is possible that the Welsh on its western boundaries were keeping his hands more than full. But

Algar, a brave young ealderman, assembled the men of the district, some three hundred in all. Two hundred more joined him, a great acquisition, for they were led by a monk named Tolius who, before entering the monastery of Croyland, had been a famous soldier. More men came from the neighboring country, and they went out bravely to meet the foe. At first they were more successful than they had dared to hope, for three Danish kings were slain; the pagans fled, and the Saxons pursued them to their very camp.

There was great rejoicing, for only the coming of night had prevented them from overpowering the invaders. Weary and happy, they returned to their own camp, but they were met by the report of the spies that many hundreds of the heathen, perhaps thousands, were pouring into the camp of the enemy. It was hopeless. The battle in the morning would not be a victory, but a slaughter. Should they die for naught? When early morning came, three-fourths of Algar's enthusiastic army had fled in the darkness of the night.

The others waited. What should they do? Who could blame them if they too had fled, for death only could lie before them? But no; in the earliest gray of the morning, Algar and Tolius went about from group to group of the weary men, many of them suffering from the wounds of the previous day, and tried, as best they might, to strengthen and encourage them.

"The cowards who were among us have stolen away in the darkness like foxes," said Algar. "Shall we be like them? Shall your children tell to their children's children that their fathers were among those that dared not meet the foe? What will the heathen say? They will say, 'These runaways who slink out of sight at the very thought of a Dane, there is nothing in them to fear,' and fiercer than ever before, they will fall upon our homes. We perish if we flee. We can but perish if we stay. Shall we stay?"

Shouts of renewed courage arose. Then there was quiet, for

the soldier monk Tolius had raised his hand for silence. He stood erect with uncovered head, looking straight into the faces of his soldiers.

"Do you see the tonsure?" said he. "That is in memory of the crown of thorns of Him who died for us. Will you refuse to die for Him? You fight the destroyers of your homes, the murderers of your wives; but more than that, you fight the bands of the heathen for the Christian faith. The Lord of Hosts is with us. Our God is a God that can work miracles. He will not desert His people. Trust in God—and fight like demons," said the monk of many battle-fields.

The light grew less dim. A weird chanting was heard in the Danish camp. It was the song of glory of the dead kings, recounting their many victories, their joy in the fight, and the seats of honor that they would hold in the halls of Odin. All the long, bright day they would find happiness in battle, sang the harpers; and when the night came, the Valkyrs would heal their wounds, and they would feast with the gods. Then came a wild lamentation, for the bodies of the kings had been placed on the ground with their weapons and bracelets, and the first earth was being sprinkled upon them. Quickly a great mound was built up and the Danes rode around it seven times, slowly and with downcast faces. Then came again the weird chanting: Men should see this mound, and as long as there were any heroes or children of heroes on the earth, they would point out the burial-place of the great kings and do them honor.

Meanwhile the priests in the camp of the Saxons were praying at the altars that they had built, and the men who were that day to fight for their land and for their God were receiving the sacrament, most of them for the last time. "The peace of God be with you," said the priest, as the men went forth to the battle that was to help to bring that peace.

Algar showed himself a skilful commander. He arranged his little company of heroes in the shape of a wedge, Tolius at the right, the sheriff of Lincoln at the left, while he and his men were in the centre. The men on the outside held their shields so close together that they made a wall impenetrable to the spears of their foes. The men behind them held their spears pointed out far beyond the men on the outside, who could use only their swords and pikes to protect themselves. This was a new scheme. The Danes rushed upon the little phalanx with fearful war-cries, but the Saxons stood firm. The horses were afraid of the bristling spear-points. The swords of the Danes and their heavy battle-axes were as harmless as feathers, for they could not come near enough to use them. They beat the air in their rage, but the little invincible phalanx, obedient to the word of the leader, turned now right, now left, and wherever it went, there were wounds and there was death.

The Danes were angry. The shadows were fast lengthening, and still the handful of Saxons drove them hither and thither as they would. The Danes made one more attack, then turned to flee as if routed. This was the supreme test of the Saxons, and they failed. They could fight like heroes, but when they saw their foes running from them, they ran after them like children. The commands and entreaties of their leaders were alike powerless. There was no more order or discipline. Every man was for himself. Madly they pursued. The enemies fled; but when the Saxons were crossing a little hollow, then, in the flash of a sword, the Danes came together—faced about—divided to the right—to the left. The brave little company was surrounded, and but three of the heroes of the morning survived.

These three had hurriedly consulted almost between the blows of their adversaries.

"Croyland," said they. "We can do nothing here. Let us warn the convent;" and as the shadows grew darker, they fled. They took three different directions that there might be three chances instead of one to warn the monks.

Croyland was no common monastery. Its rich, fertile lands were separated from the country about them by four rivers. Given by a king, Ethelbald of Mercia, it had been a favorite of other kings, and many and rich were the gifts that had been showered upon it. One king had sent to it his purple coronation robe to be made into priestly vestments, and the curtain that had hung at the door of his chamber, a marvellous piece of gold embroidery picturing the fall of Troy.

Ethelbald of Mercia in his persecuted youth had been guarded and instructed by Saint Guthlac, and it was over his grave that the grateful pupil had reared this convent. A visit to his tomb would heal the sick, and it was so favorite a resort for the suffering that, according to the legend, more than one hundred were often healed in one day. Pilgrims returning from Croyland were free from tolls and tribute throughout the Mercian kingdom. It was also a kind of city of refuge; and any accused man who had made his way to the monks of Croyland was safe from his pursuers as long as he remained within the space bounded by the further shores of the four rivers. Jewels and golden vessels and other gifts costly and rare were brought to this convent by its visitors until it had become one of the richest spots in the land.

It was the hour of matins, and the monks were assembled in the convent chapel, when the door was thrown open, and there stood three young men, exhausted with hunger, wounds, and their toilsome journey through the forest, over the stony hills and across soft, wet meadow land. Accustomed as the monks were to the coming of fugitives, they saw that this was something different.

"The blessing of God be with us—and may God save us," murmured the abbot as he left the altar.

What they had feared had come upon them. The abbot Theodore took command. The treasures of the convent must be saved; they were God's property, not theirs. With a burning eagerness to do what might be their last service, the monks set to work. Gold and silver, and brazen vessels were dropped into the well. The table of the great altar was covered with plates of gold, and that, too, was sunk into the water; but it was too long to be hidden, and so it was returned to the chapel. Chalices of gold, hanging lamps set with precious stones and hung with heavy chains of gold, jewels, muniments, charters, were piled into the boats, and then most reverently they bore to the landing-place the embalmed body of Saint Guthlac and with it his little well-worn psalter.

"Row to the south and hide yourselves and our treasures in the wood of Ancarig," said the abbot as quietly as if this was but an everyday proceeding.

"We will return swiftly," said the rowers, seizing the oars.

"You will *not* return," said the abbot in a tone of command. The young men sprang to their feet and leaped ashore.

"Then we stay to die with you," they said firmly. The abbot stood unmoved.

"I command you to go. The convent will be razed. You who are young and strong must rebuild it. The church needs you, the land needs you. Go." Not a man stirred.

"I and the old and helpless and the little children of the choir will remain. Perchance the heathen will spare those who offer no defense," said the abbot, with a faint smile. The young men only turned their steps toward the convent gate.

"Back!" thundered the abbot. "I am your superior. Where are your vows of obedience? I command you to leave me. Do you dare to disobey?" Slowly, one by one, the young men entered the boats and grasped the oars. The abbot raised his hand in blessing. He looked after them with one long, tender look, as they rowed away silently and with downcast faces. Then he hid his face in his robe and sobbed.

"My children, O my children!"

It was only a moment that he could give to his grief, for much remained to be done. He and the old men and the little boys of the choir put on their vestments. The service of the day was completed; they had partaken of the consecrated bread. Then they sang, old men with faint, quavering voices, and little boys with their fearless treble. High rose the chant as the courage of God filled their hearts.

"I will not be afraid for ten thousands of the people that have set themselves against me round about;" and again:—

"I will lay me down in peace and take my rest; for it is thou, Lord, only, that makest me dwell in safety."

The safety was not the safety of this world, for long before the psalter was ended, the Danes had burst in at the open doors. For a moment even they were awed by the calmness of the old men and the unearthly sweetness of the voices of the children; but it was only a moment.

"Where are the jewels of the altar?" cried one. "They have hidden them from us. Kill them! Torture them! Where are your treasures?" he shouted, striking down with one blow the abbot as he knelt at the altar. It seemed hardly the twinkling of an eye before every monk had fallen, and the marble floors were slippery with their blood. The little children were cut down as ruthlessly as were the old men.

Hubba, one of the sons of Lodbrog, had struck down the prior. Beside the dead man knelt one of the children of the convent weeping bitterly. Jarl Sidroc raised his sword to kill the child, the only one in the convent that still lived.

"Kill me, if you will," said the boy, looking fearlessly up into his face. "You killed my prior." The Dane swept his sword within a hand's breadth of the boy's face, but the child did not flinch.

"The Saxon cub is brave enough to be a Dane," muttered the jarl. "Get out of that thing, and I'll make a viking of you," and he tore off the boy's convent dress and threw over him his own tunic. "Stay by me, whatever happens," he whispered. "And keep out of that man's way," and he pointed to Hubba, who was fiercely swinging his axe around his head in a mad fury of slaughter.

"There are no more living. Take the dead!" shouted Hubba, and with bars and ploughshares and mattocks they broke open the tombs of the saints, piled up their embalmed bodies and set fire to them.

Many days later, while the ruins of Croyland were still smoking, a half-famished child wearing a Danish tunic painfully climbed the hill from the river. The monks who had departed at the abbot's command had made their way back. They were toiling to extinguish the flames and searching for the maimed bodies of their friends, that they might bury them reverently as martyrs for their faith. They were too sadly busy to notice his approach, until the child fell with a sob into the arms of the one that was nearest, and fainted. The monks gathered around in wonder.

"It is little Brother Turgar," said one, in amazement.

"It is his spirit come back to help us and guide us," said another.

"Could it be a wile of Satan?" whispered one fearfully. "The heathen have many dealings with evil spirits." The little boy opened his eyes.

"I am Brother Turgar," he said, and then he closed them in exhaustion.

After he had eaten and rested, he told his story. The slaughter of Croyland had been repeated at the convents of Peterborough and Ely. Timidly the child had followed his captors, fearing them, but fearing the woods with their wild beasts. As the Danes were crossing the river that lay between them and the convent at Huntingdon, driving the great herds of cattle from the convents that they had already devastated, two of the heavy wagons of spoils were overturned in a deep place in the stream. Jarl Sidroc was in command, and in the confusion his little captive softly crept away and hid in the reeds that bordered the river. Hardly daring to breathe, he lay there till even his straining ears could not hear a sound of the Danes on their march.

Then he sprang up and ran to the woods. A day and a night the child of ten years was alone in the forest with only the wild beasts about him. No wonder that the monks looked upon him reverently as upon one to whom a miracle had been shown. Through the wilderness, over rough, stony ground, in the midst of briers and nettles, over long stretches of meadow land so soft that the water oozed out around his naked feet as he went, on the child ran; on, on, would it never end? Had he always been running? He hardly knew. It was like some terrible dream. At last he began to come to places that he recognized. It was his own river. It was not wide, he swam across. That was all.

A sad confirmation of his story came a day later, when the hermits of Ancarig with whom the monks of Croyland had taken refuge with their convent treasures, came to implore their aid in burying the dead of Peterborough. The wolves were upon them, they said; would their brothers help to give them Christian burial?

Never satiated with blood and pillage, the Danes pressed on into the land of East Anglia. Neither forests nor morasses delayed them in their terrible work. Soon they were in the very heart of the kingdom.

Edmund, the king, was greatly beloved by his people, but he was not a warrior. Death and destruction had been around him for months, but he had made no preparations for defense; and when the Danes came upon his land, it was his ealderman who called out the people to battle. The brave resistance was of no avail. The Danes pushed on to the very abode of the king, where he sat in patient serenity, refusing to flee, ready to be a martyr, but with no thought of being a soldier. Thinking, perhaps, that the king who would not fight would readily become their tool, they seem to have offered him a continuance of royal power if he would yield to them. He refused, and the king who would not fight could meet torture so calmly that Inguar in a rage cut off his head at a blow. Godrun, the Dane, was placed on the throne.

The Northmen were now masters of northern and eastern Britain. Part of Mercia remained, which could stand by the aid of Wessex. Wessex remained, but Wessex, if it stood at all, must stand alone; and there was now no barrier between the Danish strongholds and the land of the West Saxons.

Chapter XIV.

THE WHITE HORSE OF ASHDOWN

It was now the time of Wessex to suffer. The Danes were not sure of being able to take Mercia, for they had seen that Wessex would come to her aid; but they felt little doubt of their ability to take Wessex, for Mercia, with the Danish force on her north and east, could lend no assistance to another kingdom.

Now in Wessex the fortified town that was farthest east was Reading. It was on the Thames, and so a great force could come by boat, while one equally great was coming with almost equal swiftness by land. To strengthen their position, the Danes threw up earthworks extending from the Thames to the Kennet, the little river to the south of Reading, and in less than three days after their arrival, they sent out bands of men to plunder the country round about.

Now there had been no fighting in Wessex since the time, some ten years before, that the Danes had pillaged Winchester. Ethelwulf, the valiant ealderman of Berkshire, who with Osric of Hants had so completely routed the pirates at the mouth of the Itchen, had not forgotten how to fight. Without waiting to send for help he brought together the men of his district. It can hardly be wondered at that they were not eager to meet the Danes, who had many times their numbers, but they took the field courageously. Up and down in front of the lines rode Ethelwulf.

"Remember the fight of the Itchen," he said. "The Danes were more than we, but the Lord helped us. He divided their forces, and they ran before us like sheep. Why should we fear the heathen? The God of battles is our leader; their commander is Satan himself."

Bravely the little company went on. The first body of Danes that they met they attacked with so much vigor that the invaders were put to flight, and one of their leaders was slain.

A fiercer contest was coming. No sooner had the tidings reached Ethelred and Alfred that their foes were in Wessex than messengers were sent over the kingdom to every village, even to every little grange. They bore an arrow and a naked sword. These they held up in sight of the people, who knew their meaning only too well, and cried:—

"The enemy are upon us. Let every man leave his house and land and come. This is the word of the king," and then they turned to ride swiftly to the next town or hamlet. If any man refused to come, his land was forfeited to the king.

Neither Ethelred nor Alfred had any practical knowledge of fighting, and it is no wonder that they mistook enthusiasm for the power that could come only with experience and numbers. Without waiting for troops to come from the more distant parts of the kingdom, they set off at once to meet the Danes; and in four days after Ethelwulf's successful encounter, they were ready with all zeal and a firm belief in their own ability to drive the heathen from their land.

Ethelred had surprised those who judged him by his somewhat childish speeches and his inaction. So long as the Danes were on the farther side of the land, it seemed impossible for him to realize that they could come nearer; but when they were once within the bounds of his own kingdom, no one could have been

MESSENGERS WERE SENT ... TO EVERY LITTLE VILLAGE.

more prompt than he in getting his men together or more fearless in leading them on to the battle.

The royal forces were in front of Reading. They expected to win, for Ethelred with fewer numbers had been successful. Wild with enthusiasm, they fell upon the Danes who were outside the fortifications. These were taken by surprise and were easily overcome. The Saxon courage rose higher. It was now late in the afternoon; they would encamp in a convenient place near at hand, and in the morning there should be another battle and another victory.

The Danes were quiet within their stronghold. The Saxons were joyfully making their camp, when, like the bursting forth of a mighty river, the enemy suddenly rushed out from the fortifications and fell upon the unsuspecting Saxons. Surprised and taken at a disadvantage as they were, the Saxons wheeled about and renewed the battle so fiercely that the Danes had far from the easy victory that they had expected.

There was no special advantage of place, for the battle-field was a long stretch of level meadow lands, and success seemed now in the hands of one side, now of the other. Both sides were equally courageous, but the Danes had many more men and life-long experience in fighting, while few of the Saxons had ever been on a field of war. The wonder is not that they were finally forced to flee, but rather that they could resist so long and so determinedly.

The retreat was hardly a flight, for they withdrew to the westward in good order, though with ranks sadly thinned, to do what would have been wiser in the first place, that is, to await the arrival of more forces. Rapidly the troops came up, in companies, in straggling bands, even one by one, for there was little delaying one for another. The farther Ethelred retreated, the more powerful he grew, and when they had come to Ashdown in Berkshire, both he and Alfred believed that if they could ever oppose the invaders, it would be then. There they halted.

But the heathen were upon their track. Faster and faster they came with the whole force save the few that remained to guard Reading. On both sides the armies had been busy in throwing up earthworks. Darkness came upon them, and through the chill of the March night, the sentinels paced to and fro, and the watch-fires blazed red and angry. The soldiers, many of them exhausted by the long march, slept heavily; but there was no rest for the young leaders upon whom the new responsibility weighed so gravely. When they were before Nottingham, there may have been some small skirmishes, but aside from these, all their experience in fighting had come from the disaster of four days previously. Thinking, perhaps, more of shelter than of military advantage, they had pitched their camp near the base of a hill, while the Danish camp was at its top.

Slowly the long night passed away. As the morning began to dawn, the anxious young commanders noticed that the Danes had divided their forces into two companies, one led by two kings, the other by the jarls.

"We will gain by their experience," said Ethelred. "If our men are in one body, and we attack one of their divisions, the other will set upon us on the rear. I will take command of half of our men and meet those who are led by the kings, and do you lead the other half and meet the jarls and their men."

"The Danes are already moving," said Alfred. "They will be upon us," but Ethelred had galloped swiftly away. There was more and more movement among the Danish troops. The top of the hill was black with them. They formed in line. Alfred almost thought that he could hear their terrible battle-cries. He drew up his own men, but where was Ethelred?

Trusting the message to no one else, Alfred went at full speed in search of his brother. He came to a thick clump of trees where the temporary altar had been built. A low sound of chanting struck his ears. It was the voice of the priest.

"Ethelred—my brother—my king," he cried, "the Danes are upon us. Their lines are formed. My men are ready. A moment's delay may lose the battle." But Ethelred said quietly:

"It is the service of God. Our priest is saying prayers for us and for our men. Shall I forsake the help of God to trust in men and in weapons? It is meet that the king pray for his people."

Alfred stood for a moment helpless, then he galloped back. Directly in front of his division was a stunted thorn tree. Here the prince stopped. The Danes were above him. They were looking down. They were ready to charge. He glanced below him. There were his own men. They stood, not like the great machine that an army is to-day, but like a multitude of individuals, held together by a common purpose, but by no strong bonds of discipline. In that one glance, Alfred saw that one face was eager, another angry, another scornful. Then came the supreme moment; they raised their shields and cried:—

"Battle! battle! Lead us to the battle!" Through the young man's mind thoughts flashed like the flashing of a sword. From his higher position he could see the multitudes of the hostile ranks more clearly than could his men. Then first, he realized the great advantage of the enemy in being on higher ground. Let the Danes make the first charge, and coming from above they would be resistless. Let the Saxons realize this, and they would perhaps flee in despair. One wrong step, and the kingdom of Wessex might be in the hands of the heathen. His very lips paled. No long prayers had the young prince made that morning, but if there ever was a true prayer, it was his whispered

"God help us!" He trembled, but his voice rang clear and strong as he shouted:—

"Forward!" and with his men following dashed up the hill "like a wild boar."

Then came the terrible onslaught of the Berserkir warriors, who excited themselves to madness and fury until they were more like ferocious wolves than men. They rolled on the ground, they beat their breasts, they gnashed their teeth, they bit their shields, they howled and they screeched, until they seemed to have lost all likeness to human beings. These were in the front of the Danish lines, and horrible, indeed, was their attack. It was not fighting men, but fiends.

From Alfred's one little experience of four days previously, he and his men realized that their only hope was in keeping together. Even Berserkir could not scatter them. Men fell by hundreds on both sides. Alfred's men could not advance beyond the stunted thorn; the Danes could not make their way one step farther down the hill. The second division of the Danes was swinging around from the other side. With no orders and no leader, Ethelred's men had formed in line, and stood in a great body, ready to charge at a moment's warning. Down came the Danish forces led by the two kings, rushing headlong down the hill to get between Alfred's men and the men without a leader. The limit of Saxon self-restraint had been reached. Edmund, who had succeeded Alstan as bishop of Sherborne, came in front of the line.

"Men of Wessex," he began; but there was a cloud of dust as a horse and rider plunged furiously up the hill, tearing up the turf at every step. It was the king. In a moment he was at the head of his army.

"The blessing of God is with us," he shouted. "The Lord will save His people. Forward!" All the more madly for their restraint, the Saxons rushed upon the two kings and their men, and drove them in frantic confusion over the hill. They were almost as wild as the Berserkir themselves. The jarls had fled in a frenzy of alarm. The whole Saxon troop pursued. One of the Danish kings was slain. One after another, five of the great jarls fell. No one noticed. No one thought of them. It was a mad scramble for safety. The battle itself had lasted only three or four hours at longest; but all day long, over hill and meadow and through the forest the Saxons pursued their retreating foes, until they had been driven back to the walls of Reading. No one knows how many thousands of the invaders fell. Their bodies lay where they had been struck down, on a rock, in a brook, under a tree, in the midst of a great stretch of meadow land. Anywhere and everywhere was a feast for the wolves and the ravens, the corpses of the Danish invaders.

Far up on Ashdown Hill is the rudely outlined figure of a horse, made by cutting away the turf from the white limestone. It is so large that it spreads over nearly an acre of the hillside. Tradition says that this is the white horse, the standard of the Saxons, cut in memory of the victory of Ashdown; and for no one knows how long, it has been the custom for the people of the neighborhood to assemble every few years to celebrate with games and races and a general jubilee a day of "scouring the White Horse," that is, of clearing away the turf and bushes that may have grown over the trenches forming the outline.

The Saxons well knew that there was nothing permanent about even so complete a victory as this. The Danes had been routed, but they could return; they had lost nothing but men, and there might be thousands more on the way. Little time could the victors spare for rejoicing over the victory or even for rest. In a fortnight the Danes were ready to march out in numbers as great as ever.

This time they went to the south across the Kennet River into Hants. Ethelred and Alfred pursued in hot haste. The Saxons were not victorious, but they were strong enough to prevent the foe from carrying away booty. But of what avail was a victory when it only opened the way for another contest? More than one king would have deserted his people and crossed the seas. The refuge of Rome was always open. It was not looked upon as a cowardly thing for a Saxon king to withdraw from active life and spend his last days in the English palace in Rome. Ethelred, at least, seems to have had some little bent toward the quiet life under the shadows of the cloister; but to neither him nor Alfred did any thought come of attempting to secure a heavenly kingdom by deserting the one that had been entrusted to them on the earth.

They pressed on boldly, and two months later, at a little place called Merton, there was another engagement. The ranks of the Danes were again filled. A fierce battle was waged all day, and in spite of their smaller numbers, the Saxons held their own. Just before sunset, the enemy made one last, furious charge, and the Saxons were forced to retreat. The brave bishop who had succeeded Alstan was slain, and the king was so severely wounded that he died soon after the battle.

Ethelred was buried with royal honors at Wimborne, but scant time could the younger brother spare for his grief. Weighty questions were pressing upon him. Must he become king? He was not yet twenty-three; he was afflicted with a painful disease whose attacks might come upon him at any moment. He had not a relative in the land, saving the children of his brothers and his sister Ethelswitha. No wonder that he repeated his childish plaint, "They all go away from me."

Is it any marvel that he fell into utter discouragement? Nominally the king of the West Saxons was king of all England, but in reality his power was limited to a part of the land of Wessex. He was at the head of the army, but the very flower of his army had fallen. Ethelwulf, upon whom he might have depended for counsel, had been slain at Reading; Osric had died long before. The Danish power was all around him. Could he accept the throne? Was there any throne to accept? Had he any country to rule? After his talk with Alstan, it had all seemed easy. He had felt strong and confident, but now he was discouraged and almost hopeless. There was no one to counsel him. The glad courage that had come to him after his lonely night in the chapel in Cornwall had left him; but he remembered his resolution and the promise that he had made to Alstan, "I will do the best that I can for my people;" and so it was that Alfred became king of England.

It was a sad coming to the throne. There was no public rejoicing, no coronation ceremonies, not even a formal declaration on the part of the counselors that they accepted him as their king; but no one thought of any opposition, and one month after Ethelred's death the Saxon soldiers met the enemy as enthusiastically as ever, at Wilton, not far from the centre of Wessex. The story of the battle was only an old tale repeated; for the Saxons fought fiercely, but were overcome at last by the same old trick of the Danes,—their pretending to be routed and then, when the ranks of the eager pursuers had lost all semblance of form and order, of wheeling about and cutting them down without mercy. It was a sad beginning for a young king's reign, but a few months later the Danes withdrew from Wessex.

The explanation seems to be that though the Danes were fighters, and though they sang many war-songs, they did not often fight without an object. So long as there were rich pastures full of flocks and herds, and churches with their treasures, to be had almost for the taking, why should they stay in Wessex where every step was marked with blood rather than gold? They moved to the east and took up their winter quarters in London.

For a year or more there was peace; then came a day when Ethelswitha fled to Alfred and said:—

"My husband can no longer meet the Danes. He has left his kingdom and gone to Rome. I cannot leave my people." This was in 874. Mercia had fallen into Danish hands, Alfred alone resisted. How long could his resistance last? Successful battles were nothing, when in a few days reËnforcements filled up the ranks of their foes. Was there any way to shut off these fresh supplies?

Now, though of the same blood as the Danes and born with the same love of the sea, the Saxons who had come to Britain had settled down to a quiet life on the land. Could the old success and fearlessness on the ocean be aroused? King Alfred pondered long and carefully, then he sent for his counselors.

"Let us," he said, "build ships that we may meet the heathen on the water, and guard the harbors and the mouths of the rivers."

At first the counselors saw many objections to the plan. They had no practised builders of ships, they had no sailors, no commanders. The Danes would be as invincible on the sea as on the land. It would be a useless waste of the energy that ought to go to defend their country.

The king bit his lip and there was a spot of anger on his cheeks.

"What will you do?" he said quietly, though there was a certain restraint in his voice that made every word tell like a blow. "We have tried to defend our land. Your brothers and sons have fallen. King Ethelred gave up his life trying to protect you. What have we gained? At the cost of many lives, we have gained a short freedom from the heathen. You well know how little a treaty with them means. They will come again in the summer, and perhaps in greater numbers than ever. You say we have no shipbuilders?

We have builders of small vessels. I can teach them to build larger ones. I can train sailors, and I can command the war-ships. What will you do?" The counselors hesitated.

"They say that the king could build a whole war-ship himself," whispered one of the counselors to another, "that he has read about them in his books."

"What will you do?" repeated the king almost sternly. His quiet confidence gave them courage, and perhaps, indeed, they felt half afraid to oppose him. They meditated a little time and then said:—

"We will build the boats."

Alfred had not fought the Danes without learning something of their military tactics. "He who would win must surprise" was one great lesson, and with this thought in mind, he planned to build his ships in a hidden recess of the rocky shore, a long arm of the sea that made an abrupt turn to the east. Projecting cliffs hid it from all but the keenest, most watchful eyes. It was a small fleet of small vessels that he built, and it was commanded by an admiral who was utterly without practical experience; but he had one great advantage. The vikings, cruising fearlessly along the southern coast, had no thought of meeting the slightest opposition until they were far inland, and when Alfred's ships suddenly appeared before them, it seemed to the superstitious pirates almost as if supernatural aid had been given to their opponents. One of the Danish ships was captured and the other six sailed back to Denmark. The enthusiasm of the hero-worshipping Saxons was aroused. They were ready to do whatever their wonderful young king might suggest, and enough of their old love of the sea came back to them to make them more than ready to build as many more vessels as Alfred thought best.

The Danes began to feel something a little like dread of the leader of the Saxons. He had won a great battle on land, and they, the invincible warriors, had been driven over field and through forest to seek refuge as best they might. Now, came this victory on the sea. That they, the rulers of the ocean, should be overpowered and forced to flee across the waters to their own land with vessels empty of treasures, was a humiliation that was new to them. They would come again, this should not be the end. The lord of the West Saxons should feel their vengeance.

Chapter XV.

Thor or Thealfi?

Three Danish kings and their forces had wintered in East Anglia, and the land had been so completely subdued that not the least resistance was made. Early in the spring of 876 they set forth on a march to their vessels. They embarked and sailed to the south. They passed the mouth of the Thames, went through Dover Straits, and bore to the westward.

The people of Kent breathed more freely, but Alfred well knew that a time of bitter trial was coming to Wessex. Nearer the ships came. Where would the first blow be struck? The Danes now expected to meet the Saxon fleet; and unless possibly with the advantage of surprise, it could not hope to oppose them, hardly to delay them long enough to warrant even a small portion of the loss that was sure to be the final result.

Still westward came the pirates. They passed the Isle of Wight and entered the wide bay at the east of Dorsetshire. They landed near Wareham, seized the fortress with hardly a struggle, and in a very short time had thrown up earthworks and made a place of safety for themselves.

The king of Wessex had not been idle. The Danes, probably expecting the arrival of the Saxons by sea, had made their defenses especially strong on the seaward side. Alfred marched around to the west. His ranks were thin, for it was earlier in the season than the Danes were wont to sally forth on their expeditions, and it was not easy to collect men at this time. He did the only thing that gave the least promise of success, and attacked the companies that were making their raids outside the fortifications.

Both sides had learned from the previous encounters. The Danes retreated to their defenses, and Alfred was now too wise to attack fortifications that were too strong for him. It was the situation at Nottingham repeated. The Danes could not come out, and the Saxons could not go in. The outcome was precisely the same. A parley was held and a treaty was made.

Alfred well knew of how little value a treaty was in the eyes of the heathen, but there was a possibility of gaining time, and as a last resort he determined to make the mutual agreement in the way that would be most binding upon his own people, hoping that the solemnity with which the Saxons would make their promises would produce some effect upon the heathen.

The Danes built up an altar and made sacrifices of many beasts. A golden bracelet which had been taken in battle was made red with the sacred blood and laid upon the altar. The kings and jarls marched slowly around it, and finally each one laid his hand upon the bloody ring, and swore for himself and the men under his command that they would withdraw from the land of Wessex, doing no harm to man, woman, child, or property.

The most binding oaths known to the Saxons were those sworn on the relics of the saints; so Alfred had collected from the churches and convents that had not been pillaged, bones of the saints, their scourges, robes, psalters, and any other articles that had belonged to them. Other relics had been brought from secret places, from forests and swamps and dens in the rocks, where they had been hastily concealed at the rumors of the Danes' approach. With much ceremony the king and his chief men laid their hands upon these relics, and promised that there should be no molestation of the Danes, if they would withdraw peaceably from the land of the Saxons.

Each nation had sworn by the most sacred form of oath known to them, and now the Danes even offered to confirm their good faith by taking another oath on Alfred's relics. Half fearfully the superstitious heathen touched the pile, not quite knowing what might happen. They took the oath again, gave many hostages, and withdrew into the fortifications to prepare to leave the land.

A few nights later they were holding a feast. The cup went around many times, passing with careful equality of treatment from soldier to king and from king to soldier.

"It is not the way of the vikings to leave so goodly a land rich in convents and churches and go away as poor as they came," said one of the jarls.

"We have sworn by Thor," said another. "If we break an oath to Thor, he will strike us with his hammer and send us to the land of the forgotten." The first jarl broke into a hilarious laugh.

"You think you swore by Thor, do you, children that you are? Leave the seas and plant corn, that is all that you are good for." The men sprang to their feet. The jarl only laughed again, and looked at them with contempt.

"It is well that there is one among you," said he, "who is not a child. You think you swore by Thor?" and again he laughed, a wild, scornful, triumphant laugh. "Let me tell you. When the soothsayer said the words that made the blood of the beasts sacred to Thor, he said not the name of Thor, but of Thealfi. I saw to that. One among you is wise." The vikings' faces grew eager, and the men pressed nearer.

"Are you afraid of Thealfi, the servant of Thor?" he asked.

"No, no, no," they shouted.

"Are you afraid of a pile of old clothes and bones?" he went on.

Here they hesitated. The solemnity of the Saxons had not been without its effect upon them. The jarl watched their faces.

"I was at Croyland," he said, "and after there were no more to kill, we piled up the bodies of the saints, scores of them, and burned them. They made a bonfire that was as glorious as the rising sun," he added quietly, and turned to the great cup of mead. That they had given hostages was nothing to them, and with wild shouts they sallied forth, murdered the Saxon horsemen whom Alfred had left on guard, seized their horses, and swept in a devastating course across the land to the westward, burning and pillaging and murdering as they went. Alfred was not near enough to intercept them in their headlong march. They came to Exeter and fortified it.

The Danes now held two strongly protected harbors on the southern shores of Wessex, and all through that winter the pirate fleets cruised fearlessly along the coast, putting into either of the retreats whenever they chose to ravage the land and fill their vessels with Saxon plunder. Finally the Danes decided to bring their forces together at Exeter. The war-ships were loaded and they set sail for the west.

Alfred was in camp before Exeter. He was not strong enough to overpower the Danes, but he could keep them from further invasion of the land round about. He heard of the sailing of the Danish ships, one hundred and twenty of them, great war-galleys loaded almost to the water's edge with the plunder that they had collected at Wareham. He did not dare to leave his station, but he ordered his fleet to put to sea. Little more than one hundred miles away were the vikings, but a strong west wind prevailed, and with their loaded vessels they could only beat and beat and make no real headway. For nearly one month the Danes, who claimed that winds and waves were their allies, were driven up and down at their mercy.

WHEN THEY TRIED TO CLIMB UP THE LOFTY SIDES IT WAS AN EASY MATTER FOR THE SAXONS TO THRUST THEM DOWN.

Surely the elements were on the side of the Saxons, for when they met some of the Danish ships, the waves ran so high that the Danes could not follow their usual custom of lashing their boats to the enemy's for the fight. Moreover, their vessels were low in the water, and Alfred's stood high, so that the Danish arrows were almost harmless, and when they tried to climb up the lofty sides, it was an easy matter for the Saxons to thrust them down with their spears. The other Danish boats were out of sight, no one knew where, for a dense fog had settled down upon the sea; and when the fog was driven away, it was by a strong south wind that drove the pirate vessels upon rocks far more fierce than their enemies. Nearly all the Danish ships went to the bottom.

The Danes in Exeter sued most humbly for peace. The counselors, elated by their easy victory at sea, advised an instant attack upon the garrison at Exeter; but Alfred, the impetuous fighter of Ashdown, was the one to hesitate.

"We could attack them," he argued, "and perhaps kill the whole number, but they would fight desperately. We should lose many of our men, and while we have few to fill up our ranks, they have hordes. They have almost all England," he said sadly. The counselors were silent. King Alfred went on:—

"They have help near at hand. Hubba and the raven standard are in Wales. I have heard that he is jealous of King Guthrum, but in the last extremity they would stand together."

"Then if we let Guthrum go, will they not unite and come down upon us?" asked one of the counselors.

"I fear it," said the king. "I know that it seems only a question whether it is better to risk immediate destruction, or destruction only a little delayed; but it seems to me wiser to delay. Perhaps before the next season we can strengthen our army. The robbers that we hired fought well for us on the sea; it may be that we can hire men to fight with us on the land."

The counselors could but admit the truth of the king's words. Again a treaty was made, gravely and mechanically on the part of the Saxons, and with earnest protestations of good faith on the part of the Danes.

The enemy withdrew quietly into Mercia, and the poor, ravaged Saxon land hoped for at least a winter of peace; but soon after the Christmas of 877, the forces of Guthrum swept down from the north, the men of Hubba came up from the south, Chippenham was made their headquarters, and the whole district was overrun.

Alfred had now been on the throne for seven years, seven years of constant anxiety and struggling. He had fought bravely, but the great numbers of the Danes had made his bravery of little avail. He had won victories, but they had only opened the way for defeats. He had driven the enemy from one corner of his land only to see them return to another part of it in greater numbers, and with the fury of men who had an injury to avenge. With no guide but that of an experience that was growing more and more bitter every day; with no counselors whose knowledge was at all to be compared with his own, young as he was; with an army thinned beyond all possibility of further self-defense; with great numbers of his people driven away to foreign lands by the want of food; and worst of all, with a people whose enthusiasm had gone, whose faces were sad and hopeless, and who had lost their first earnest confidence in their leader,—what was left for the king to do?

Sadly he thought over his past life. He remembered the day that the Danes had taken Winchester, and how sure he had been that if he had been there, he could have done "something." He remembered the trust of Alstan in him and his own promise, "What is for the good of my people shall ever be first with me." Had he been overbearing with them, impatient with their ignorance? What could he do for them? The Danes would never cease trying to overcome him. He could not defend his people; would it not be better if he disappeared from among them? The treasures of the land were gone, there was little reason for further pillage. Without him, it might be that the Danes and the Saxons would come to live together in peace. Whither could he go? Suicide was the refuge of a coward. Rome? He could not live there in plenty, leaving his abandoned people in want.

The next morning King Alfred had disappeared. A faithful little band of friends had gone with him, and his wife and family soon followed. He had taken refuge, not in the luxuries of Rome, but in the marshy wilderness of Somerset. The king who had grown up in the plenteousness of the royal houses was often faint with hunger.

This swampy forest was not without its dwellers, men who cared for the swine or the cattle of some landholder. They had built themselves rude huts of brushwood plastered with mud, or of earth mixed with straw. The most luxurious among these homes were made by setting up posts in a circle, interweaving twigs of hazel and filling the spaces with clay. The roof was made of poles, and was clumsily thatched with straw. When the smoke went out—if it went out at all—it had to find its way through the door or through a hole in the roof.

In such huts as these the king took refuge. One of these men was a herdsman of his own; but the faithful servant kept the secret even from his wife, who could not understand why her husband was feeding an idle, helpless fellow. The story is that she tried to make the worthless idler useful and set him to watch some cakes that were baking before the fire. When she returned, the king sat gazing absently at the blaze and the cakes were smoking. She scolded him roundly. The old ballad, puts it:—

> "There, don't you see the cakes are burnt?
>   Then wherefore turn them not?
>   You're quick enough to eat them
>   When they are good and hot."

One by one, many men learned where the king had hidden himself. His household could hardly have come to him without several being in the secret. The little band of refugees in the forest grew larger. Their food was the fish from the rivers and the animals that they shot with their bows and arrows. They urged Alfred to return, and to call upon the men of Wessex to rally around his standard.

"No," he said. "The time may come when we shall be strong enough; it is not yet here. The Danes cannot attack us in these bogs and marshes, and we can sally out by night wherever we can find a camp. They themselves shall furnish us food."

But there must be a place of abode a little more permanent than this flitting from swamp to swamp, and Alfred chose with the greatest care a small island containing about two acres of ground. All around it were dense thickets of alder, so similar that only one very familiar with the country could hope to find his way among them. These were of themselves almost concealment enough; but Athelney, as Alfred named his island, was in a district overflowed by the river Parret. Twice a day the "bore" swept up the stream, making the peat-bogs and the swamps into broad lagoons. Here it was that the king in exile built his fortifications and trained the men who were coming to him day by day until the little island was crowded with the faithful band.

In all his dangers King Alfred had carried in his bosom the

little book of psalms and prayers that Swithin had given him. The legend is that one day he and his wife and a single thegn were alone on the island, for the others had gone to fish. He was reading aloud from this book, when a needy man suddenly appeared before him and begged for food and drink for Christ's sake. There was but a single loaf of bread and a little wine, but Alfred remembered the time when he had not even so much, and he shared them with the beggar. Then the king turned again to his book and fell asleep. He dreamed that Saint Cuthbert came to him and said:—

"It is I who have been your guest. Your trouble is near its end, and in token of this your men will bring home fish enough for an army."

Sure enough, the men did have an enormous haul of fish; but in spite of any visions that may have come to Alfred, these months of waiting, he hardly knew for what, were very trying to heart and mind. At such times, a new sorrow, however small, seems more than one can bear; and when the king found that the slender gold chain had snapped and his jewel was lost, he felt as if all hope had gone with it. To his little son he said:—

"Edward, if your mother had gone away from you forever, and you had lost the last thing that she gave you, what should you do?"

"I'd be sorry," said the child, looking up with quick sympathy. But Alfred's wife said:

"My husband, you told me once that when she gave it to you, she said that one day you would lose it, but that you must not grieve, for then the hardest days of your life would have passed. Good news will come." The king shook his head with a smile, but he felt a new courage in spite of all his wise reasoning against superstition.

Elswitha was triumphant when the very next day there shone a bright gleam of hope. Hubba, the last of the sons of Ragnar Lodbrog, had suddenly landed in Devon, bringing with him the magical flag whereon was the raven that spread its wings gleefully whenever the Danes were to win the day. The ealderman Odda had contrived to surprise the invaders. Hubba was slain, but what brought much more distress and even dismay to his followers, the raven flag had been captured.

More and more encouraging grew the reports that were brought to Alfred by way of the slender bridge that he had built over the Parret. His followers believed that should the king but name a rallying place, a great army would assemble to fight under his standard. The most careful estimates were made of the number that could be depended upon to come; then of the number of the heathen that were in and about Chippenham.

To this time belongs the legend that the king would trust none but his own eyes to count his foes, and he resolved to visit their camp. The minstrel of whatever nation was free to wander where he would, and was sure of a hearty reception in any camp or at any court. In the garb of a harper Alfred and a single attendant made their way through Selwood Forest, testing their disguise at some of the scattered manors on their road. An uproarious welcome greeted them at the Danish camp. The king sang to his foes and amused them with his jests and tricks, until he had learned all that he wanted to know of the number of the Danes and the strength of their fortifications. Then he returned joyfully to his island, and sent forth the arrow and the naked sword.

The second week in May of 878 was the time appointed for the assembling of the Saxon forces. "And when they saw the king, alive after such tribulations," says the old chronicle, "they received him as he merited, with joy and acclamation."

There were few moments of delay, even for "joy and acclamation." If Alfred would win, he must surprise. There was one night's rest, for many had marched long distances, and then came the great battle of Ethandune. In three days Alfred was again a king, for the remnant of the Danes were shut up in their fortress, with little food and no hope of reËnforcements. In two weeks they surrendered, begging for peace on any terms that the king would grant.

They made the usual offer of hostages and of their most solemn oaths; but there was one thing that was new, Guthrum avowed his willingness and that of his men to receive Christian baptism. Now to the heathen tribes of the north the acceptance of baptism indicated a wish to give up the wild life of the viking and to settle down quietly on the land. Alfred saw many proofs of the sincerity of the warriors, and a few weeks after the surrender, Guthrum and thirty of his chief men were baptized, and around their heads was bound the white linen cloth that they were to wear for eight days in token of the baptismal purifying.

During this time they were guests of the king, and then it was that they made their agreement upon what terms they should live together. Alfred granted to them East Anglia, the northern half of Mercia, and Northumbria, retaining a kind of overlordship. The penalty for injury done, whether to Saxon or to Dane, was to be the same.

Again Alfred was on the throne, but over what a kingdom he ruled! In all these years of fighting, the marauders had run at large throughout the land. Hardly a corner of it had been free from them. Over and over, crops had been burned, until in some districts agriculture had been entirely given up. The churches with their treasures had been pillaged and destroyed. The monastery of Peterborough had been collecting books for two centuries; and these were swept away, as was the library of every other convent that had felt the Danish touch. The convents were the seats of the schools; and these were gone, and the monks killed or driven into exile. There was no full treasury and the revenues must all be built up. The fortifications were in ruins. There was no strong band of counselors to advise and coöperate with him. There was no strong band of young men to carry out his will. Worst of all, perhaps, was the feeling of unrest and distrust that was the natural result of so many years of danger and uncertainty. Alfred stood alone. The problem was: Given, a devastated land, an empty treasury, an ignorant, unsettled people, and one strong, wise, conscientious man, to build up a nation.

Chapter XVI.

In Time of Peace

However fully Alfred may have trusted the Danes, he was wise enough to know that his first duty was to make himself able to defend his country if they should prove unworthy of his trust. The Saxon fortifications were in ruins, and they had never been of any real value unless strengthened by the Danes, for not once had the heathen been repulsed from them. They must be repaired. He laid his plans before his counselors.

"Let us," he said, "if it seems good to you, let us build a line of forts around our coast, that we may be protected against our foes if they come by sea." Alfred well knew the slowness of his people to take in a new idea, but yet he was surprised at not receiving the eager encouragement that he had expected. At last one counselor said:—

"Men ought to look after their land and their homes; the harvest time is near."

"But if the Danes should come upon us and destroy the harvest?" said Alfred. "I have some confidence that Guthrum is sincere, but there are many other leaders. There is a rumor even now that Hasting will try to persuade him to join in another attack."

"Then we can meet them as we met Guthrum," said one.

"Can we?" asked Alfred quietly. "We brought out the whole strength of our land. The Danes have men without number to call on. Could we have won if their forces had been doubled?"

Slowly the counselors agreed, and slowly but surely the whole body of the people came around to the king's ideas. On his own lands forts rose rapidly, on the lands of the kingdom more slowly; for Alfred's notion of the duty of a king was that as far as possible he should lead his people and not drive them. Then too, he was anxious to introduce the use of stone in building, and for this he must hire men from abroad to teach his workmen, and it could not be done in a day or in a year; but the king was patient and persevering, and when the time of need came again, Wessex was safe.

London had long been in the hands of the Danes, and it was eight years after the conquest of Guthrum before Alfred felt it wise to rebuild it. It had been pillaged and burned, and among the ruins and in such huts as they had built for themselves lived wild crowds of adventurers and lawless men of every nation. Alfred really had to march out with a band of soldiers to capture his own city; but it yielded easily, and in the hands of the royal force of native and foreign builders, it soon lost its desolate appearance.

There must be a strong navy, and with the ideas that Alfred had adopted from the Danes and the Frisians, he could now make many improvements upon his earlier attempts at ship-building, and it was not many years before there were at least one hundred war-galleys fully equal to those of his enemies.

Alfred formed a code of laws for his people, a combination of the Golden Rule, the Ten Commandments, the laws of Moses, and the ancient laws of the land, modified and adapted to the circumstances of his people. He had a way of inquiring into the decisions of his judges that must have been discouraging to an unjust magistrate, and once he even hanged one of his own judges for condemning a man without the consent of the jury. His justice was so well known that it was almost sure proof of a man's innocence if he begged for a trial before the king.

Besides forts and ships and cities, there was other "edifying" that he must attend to, for while in his great distress on Athelney he had vowed that if he was ever restored to his kingdom, he would build a monastery on the island. Then he built a convent in Shaftesbury for women, and when it was known that the king's daughter was to be its abbess, there were many noble ladies ready to enter its gates with her. Many churches he rebuilt and repaired; but this was much easier than to find clergy for them, for Alfred's teachers of the people must not be ignorant men. He himself says that when he came to the throne, there was not a priest south of the Thames who could translate a page of Latin into Saxon, and there had been no opportunity for matters to improve.

The only way was to persuade learned men from other countries to come to him. Among these was one Grimbald, a French priest of high repute, and to his archbishop Alfred sent an embassy with generous gifts, praying that he would permit Grimbald to come to England. The archbishop was much flattered by the request, and sent a letter agreeing to the king's wishes. In this letter he thanks his royal petitioner for his gift of hounds to "control" the wolves that were such a pest in France; and then delights himself in manufacturing an elaborate comparison between the protecting hounds and the priest who was to become a spiritual watchdog to keep evil from the English church.

Alfred's well-known love of justice was the means of bringing to him the friend whom he seems to have found most congenial, Asser, a Welsh priest. Now a certain bishop of western Wales had been driven out of his diocese and his monastery plundered by a Welsh prince who had sworn allegiance to Alfred. This bishop was sure that the just king would punish such conduct if it was known to him, and he persuaded his kinsman, Asser, to undertake the wearisome journey of more than two hundred miles, for Alfred and his court were then in Sussex.

There was no delay in getting access to the king, and Asser well knew how to tell a story briefly and clearly. Hardly interrupting their conversation, Alfred sent an emphatic message by a swift courier to the Welsh prince.

"If you wish for the aid of the king of the Saxons against the six sons of Rotri, restore Novis to his diocese, and repay him twofold for all injury done to his church or to his monastery."

Question after question the king asked of the priest, about Wales, the people, the churches, what treasures of books they possessed; and then Asser must tell him of the books that he had read and what they were about. In this eager conversation the whole day passed. The shadows began to lengthen, and still the king questioned. Suddenly he said:—

"You are weary and you shall rest, but first tell me one thing more. You are the man that I want. Will you stay with me and be my friend and help me to help my people? I will give you far more than you possess beyond the Severn. Will you stay?" Alfred was used to judging men and to making his decisions in a moment on the battlefield, and he knew his man at a glance; but Asser was used to solitude and quiet and plenty of time to think over matters.

"Do not think that I am ungrateful," he said, "but I cannot change my life in a moment. You offer me greater honors and greater wealth than I ever thought of possessing, but my people are in Wales. There I was brought up and educated, and there I received the tonsure and was ordained. I cannot think that I ought to abandon my home." The king looked disappointed, but in a moment he said eagerly:—

"Then come to me for six months in each year," but the cautious Asser replied:—

"I must consult my friends. I cannot promise even that so hastily." Alfred urged, and at last Asser agreed to return after six months with a reply which the king was shrewd enough to see would probably be satisfactory.

Poor Asser was taken ill on the way home, and could not return to the king as he had promised. Alfred had been impatiently waiting, and when the day came and did not bring the priest, royal messengers were sent to hasten his journey. More than six months longer passed before Asser could leave his sick-bed, but then he went directly to Alfred; for the Welsh priests had decided, as Alfred expected, that it would be of advantage to their church to have one of their number at the king's court.

The six months passed all too rapidly for the king and too slowly for the priest; for in spite of the king's kindness and the lavish presents that he was every day giving to the priest, and in spite of the learned man's pleasure in reading and conversing with so eager a pupil, the poor exile was undeniably homesick. The six months were gone. Week after week went by. Many times Asser begged to go, but always the king put him off with some excuse. At last Christmas was near, and Asser made up his mind to demand leave to go home, and when the king sent for him on Christmas Eve, he went with his speech all prepared. He had no chance to deliver it, for the king met him with a smile and held out two sheets of parchment for him to read. On them were long lists of the treasures in two monasteries, one in Wilts and one in Wessex.

"This is your Christmas gift," said the king; and he added a silken pall of great value and as much incense as a strong man could carry.

"I have many more gifts for you," said Alfred, "but now visit your monasteries and your own country, and then come back to me. An escort is waiting to attend you. Farewell, and do not fail me."

Long before this Alfred had established schools and restored convents, so that his people might have the advantages that had been denied to him. He insisted that all the free young folk of his kingdom should learn to read Saxon, and that all who had ability and could give more time to study should go on and learn Latin, which was the book-language of the day. Doubtless some of Alfred's people were a little shocked when they found that the king's son was taught to read even before he learned to hunt. The poor old ealdermen who had fought so bravely with Alfred had rather a hard time of it, for, as they acted as judges in their districts, it would not do to have them ignorant of the laws and their meaning. The old fighters strove courageously and would often lament that they had not had in their youth the opportunities that their sons were having. Many of them gave up the terrible struggle with the alphabet. They could conquer the Danes, but not the a, b, c; and for them Alfred appointed teachers to read and talk to them and tell them the wonderful things that were in books.

But Alfred was to do much more to teach his people than even to open schools. Few would ever go further in their education than to learn to read Saxon, and there were not many Saxon books. The king must not only build the schools, he must prepare the books, and the way it came about was this. Some three years after Alfred's first acquaintance with Asser, the two men were sitting in the king's chamber holding one of their long talks about all sorts of things, and Asser chanced to read the king a sentence that he particularly liked.

"I must remember that," said Alfred. "Will you write it in my book?" and he drew forth the little book of psalms that Swithin had given him so long ago, and that he had always carried with him. The few pages were full of psalms and prayers, and there was no room for more, so Asser hurried away to get another parchment, and folded it into convenient form.

"Write it fast," said the impatient king, for poor Asser was too anxious to give a good specimen of the writing done in the book-room of his monastery.

"Why can't I translate this into Saxon and give it to my people?" asked the king eagerly; and before Asser could answer, Alfred was saying over the Latin to himself and putting it, word by word, into simple, everyday Saxon.

"Now read me more," he said, and in the course of that one day he found three other quotations that pleased him. The priest must write these in the little book "fast," and the king would hardly wait till they had been written before he began to translate them from Latin to Saxon. So it was that Alfred began to be an author.

Asser's love had been won very slowly, but when the king had once gained it, the Welsh priest was his friend forever, and it is Asser himself who has told us this story of Alfred's first beginning of book-making for his people.

Alfred does not seem to have hesitated about which books were of most value. First he translated a letter of Pope Gregory's that was written to teach bishops how to do the most that they could for their dioceses. Then came a book about the Saxons' own land, written by a monk named Bede. It was two hundred years old in Alfred's time, and he added to it whenever he knew more of any subject than Bede had known. This is the famous old book that says there are no snakes in Ireland, and it goes even farther, for it says that if any one is bitten by a serpent and is given to drink a little of the scrapings of an Irish book put into water, he will recover.

The book that must have taken him longest, and which, I fancy, is the one that interested him most, is a work by a Spaniard called Orosius, who lived about five hundred years before Alfred. It is a kind of history and geography combined. Alfred translates and explains. When he comes to the description of Sweden, he leaves Orosius and writes what Othere, one of his own sea-captains, has told him of the country. Longfellow has made a poem of the story:—

> "Othere, the old sea-captain,
>   Who dwelt in Helgoland,
> To King Alfred the Lover of Truth,
> Brought a snow-white walrus tooth,
>   Which he held in his brown right hand.
>
> * * * * *
>
> "And Alfred, King of the Saxons,
>   Had a book upon his knees,
> And wrote down the wondrous tale
> Of him who was first to sail
>   Into the arctic seas."

Then Longfellow goes on and tells the story of Othere's wonderful voyage to the North Cape, almost in the sea-captain's own words.

Alfred translated other books and persuaded his bishops to follow his example. In his translating, he never forgot that he was working to teach his people, and if the passage was not clear he would write a little more to explain it. If there was an illustration that he thought they would not understand, he would leave it out and put in one of his own. To one of his books there is a little preface which seems to have been written by some one else at his dictation. It ends by asking that, if any read it who know more than he, they will not blame him for his mistakes, for he has done as well as he could.

Alfred was performing the duties of king, warrior, statesman, teacher, author, builder of forts and churches and convents and ships. With his instinct for seizing upon what was of value to him in everything, he made up his mind to imitate the systematic life of the cloister not only in dividing his time, but in the use that he made of his money. He determined that half his time and half his money should go to the special service of God. To divide his money was not difficult, to divide his time in those clockless days was not so easy; but when a thing was to be done, Alfred, king of the Saxons, could always find a way. On clear days there was no trouble, for he could tell the progress of time by the progress of the sun; so he found how long a candle must be in order to burn four hours. Six candles, then, would burn just one day and night, and by marking each candle into twelve spaces, he could divide his time into periods of twenty minutes each.

There was one difficulty which he had not foreseen. Even the king's palace was so full of draughts that no corner of it could be found sufficiently sheltered to prevent the candles from burning unequally, and the king saw that he was not dividing his time as exactly as he had thought. His next idea was to surround the candles with thin sheets of horn, making a sort of lantern, and poor, admiring Asser, ignorant of the merits of plate glass, says with enthusiasm that the candles shone just as brightly without as within.

Once more the Danish pirates made an attempt to subdue the king. In 893 a leader named Hasting came to Kent with a great force. He made one camp in northern Kent and another near the southern shore. His plan seems to have been to slip through the forest and attack Winchester or Reading. The king was well prepared, and for one year the enemy did little but to send out an occasional marauding party.

The Danes of northern and eastern England had been growing more and more uneasy, and the second year of the war Hasting determined to take refuge in East Anglia and collect more troops. He hoped not to meet Alfred, but the king and Prince Edward pursued, and Hasting lost a great battle. All the old love of fighting had been aroused in the Danes of the eastern coast, and crowds of them joined the pirate leader. On the east and south and west, the enemy attacked the Saxon kingdom. At every point Alfred or his son Edward or his brave son-in-law Ethelred, ealderman of Mercia, was ready for them. Twice Hasting's wife and children fell into the hands of Alfred, and twice, in spite of the protests of his ealdermen, he restored them to his foe, laden with gifts; but this generosity seems to have been lost on the pirate.

Finally, Hasting went with his fleet up the Thames and the river Lea, and built a strong fort twenty miles from London. Unfortunately for him, he was fighting with a man of inventive mind; and to this king who could make a clock of candles, the thought occurred that he could easily obstruct the river or turn it out of its course, and leave the Danish fleet on dry land. He set to work at once, but this prospect was too much for even the Danes. They saw that they were beaten, and fled, leaving their ships to the mercy of the Saxons. There were small uprisings after this, but practically the land was at peace.

Four years of quiet happiness in the kingdom that he had built up remained to the king. His dearly loved sister Ethelswitha had gone over sea and land that she might spend her last days in Rome and be buried beside her husband. Before reaching Rome she died, but save for this loss there was not a shadow over the family life of the king. His wife was all that he could ask, and his children were worthy of their parents. His oldest daughter became the wife of the brave Ethelred, ealderman of Mercia; the second was abbess of a great convent; the third married a son of the Count of Flanders and the king's playmate stepmother Judith. Of Alfred's two sons, the younger showed a love of learning that was a delight to his father; and the older proved for many years before the king's death his ability to govern and protect the land of the Saxons.

In 901 Alfred died and was buried with his father at Winchester. At twenty-two he inherited a land overrun by savage pirates,—a restless, ignorant, defenseless land. The king was not safe in his palace, the priest in his church. There was little opportunity for agriculture; laws were not executed; schools had disappeared, the very wish to learn had disappeared; the whole land was rapidly sinking into ignorance and barbarism, and was exhausted by its sickening dread of the horrors that the next moment might bring.

To restore a land in such a condition to peace and quiet and safety and freedom from fear of harm, to establish churches and schools, to make just laws, and see to it that they were justly executed—a man might well have been proud to have succeeded in doing any one of these things; and for the man who brought about all these good results, no praise can be too high. To him who, in the midst of all the fighting and the weariness and the anxiety and the temptation and the responsibility, lived a calm, simple, unselfish, blameless life, to him of all the sovereigns of England who have served their country well, may the title, "The Great," most justly be given.

"I have sought to live my life worthily."

—ALFRED THE GREAT.

www.ingramcontent.com/pod-product-compliance
Lightning Source LLC
LaVergne TN
LVHW041955060526
838200LV00002B/23